"For the f...
I'm findin...

She blinked. "Cute ?...

"Really cute," he murmured.

"You're up to something, Logan."

He clucked his tongue. "So suspicious."

She shrugged. "A woman learns it young."

He realized that he had her trapped between his body and the kitchen counter. Holding her gaze, he reached out a finger and drew it along the curve of her jaw.

Her eyes narrowed and she held herself still. He could swear that stillness cost her. There was a tremor there, rigidly controlled, beneath her flawless golden skin. A quivering reaction to his presence, his touch. His heart pumped hard in his chest, but he ignored it. This was about what *he* did to Elena. His gaze dropped to the pulse beat in her throat. It was fluttering fast, he thought.

Very fast.

Dear Reader,

There's more than one way to enjoy the summer. By picking up this month's Silhouette Special Edition romances, you will find an emotional escape that is sure to touch your heart and leave you believing in happily-ever-after!

I am pleased to introduce a gripping tale of true love and family from celebrated author Stella Bagwell. In *White Dove's Promise*, which launches a six-book spin-off—plus a Christmas story collection—of the popular COLTONS series, a dashing Native American hero has trouble staying in one place, until he finds himself entangled in a soul-searing embrace with a beautiful single mother, who teaches him about roots…and lifelong passion.

No "keeper" shelf is complete without a gem from Joan Elliott Pickart. In *The Royal MacAllister*, a woman seeks her true identity and falls madly in love with a *true* royal! In *The Best Man's Plan*, bestselling and award-winning author Gina Wilkins delights us with a darling love story between a lovely shop owner and a wealthy businessman, who set up a fake romance to trick the tabloids…and wind up falling in love for real!

Lisa Jackson's *The McCaffertys: Slade* features a lady lawyer who comes home and faces a heartbreaker hero, who desperately wants a chance to prove his love to her. In *Mad Enough To Marry*, Christie Ridgway entertains us with an adorable tale of that *maddening* love that happens only when two kindred spirits must share the same space. Be sure to pick up Arlene James's *His Private Nurse*, where a single father falls for the feisty nurse hired to watch over him after a suspicious accident. You won't want to miss it!

Each month, Silhouette Special Edition delivers compelling stories of life, love and family. I wish you a relaxing summer and happy reading.

Sincerely,

Karen Taylor Richman
Senior Editor

Please address questions and book requests to:
Silhouette Reader Service
U.S.: 3010 Walden Ave., P.O. Box 1325, Buffalo, NY 14269
Canadian: P.O. Box 609, Fort Erie, Ont. L2A 5X3

Mad Enough
To Marry

CHRISTIE RIDGWAY

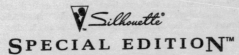

SPECIAL EDITION™

Published by Silhouette Books

America's Publisher of Contemporary Romance

For Kim, Lisa, Leila, Suzette, Tori, Wendy and Vicki,
aka "The First Grade Moms." Thanks for all the support
and the good times we've had together!

 SILHOUETTE BOOKS

ISBN 0-373-24481-9

MAD ENOUGH TO MARRY

Visit Silhouette at www.eHarlequin.com

Printed in U.S.A.

CHRISTIE RIDGWAY

thinks she has the greatest job in the world. She loves writing stories, and the only thing she loves more is her family: a supportive husband and two sons who often are forced to remind her that kids are entitled to three meals a day.

A native of California, she now lives in the southern part of the state. A typical writing day can include rescuing the turtle from the pool and finding frogs in the shower. Although she once told the men she loves they could not keep pets that require live food, each week her husband comes home with a plastic bag of pet food that looks suspiciously like crickets (sounds like them, too!) for the reptiles and amphibians that now call her home theirs.

When not writing or chasing down errant pets, she volunteers at her sons' school. Finally, because there's really nothing better, Christie always finds time to curl up with a good book.

You may contact her at P.O. Box 3803, La Mesa, CA 91944. Send a SASE for reply or e-mail her at christie@christieridgway.com.

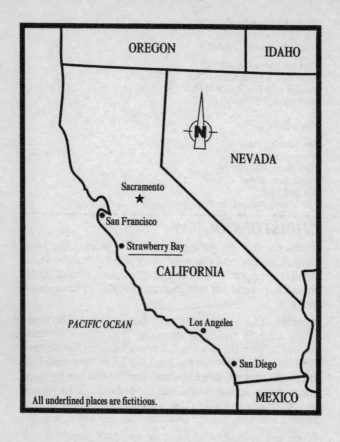

OREGON

IDAHO

NEVADA

Sacramento
★

San Francisco

● Strawberry Bay

CALIFORNIA

PACIFIC OCEAN

Los Angeles
●

● San Diego

All underlined places are fictitious.

MEXICO

Chapter One

Scandal.

Staring straight at it, Logan Chase strolled along Strawberry Bay's crowded main street, barricaded for the annual May Fair. He sighed. Over the past several months, the small California town had suffered through a series of earthquakes followed by a string of armed robberies. Why should it be any surprise that scandal was next?

Strawberry Bay, California, was, in general, a prosperous town and its citizens were always eager to support the multitude of organizations represented at the traditional community event. They lined up at the various booths, cash ready to buy the hot dogs the elementary school PTA was selling, the cinnamon rolls handmade by the Methodist Church's women's group and the cold cans of soda the kids from the high school's Key Club were hawking.

By all appearances, this year's May Fair was going to break previous fundraising records for the causes on hand, with the sole exception of the cause whose booth was situated at the far end of the street. But Logan knew it was making its own place in infamy. His gaze lingered on the booth, deserted except for the woman sitting alone inside it, even as he told himself it wasn't any of his business that she was probably already the talk of the town.

An elbow nudged his ribs. "Hey! Long time no see."

Forcing his gaze away from the mud-in-the-making, Logan looked into the freckled face of the woman who cut his hair. "How you doing, Sue Ellen?"

She wasn't any older than he was, as a matter of fact they'd sat beside each other in senior French at Strawberry Bay High School eleven years ago, but the frown she gave him was motherly. "I'm fine, but you really could use a trim."

Logan ignored the suggestion. He didn't feel like explaining why he was no longer slave to a standing monthly haircut. "How are Chris and the kids?" he asked instead.

"The twins are looking forward to summer already," Sue Ellen replied. "And my stepdaughter— you know, Chris's Amber?—she's all excited about the high school's senior prom." Sue Ellen's gaze slid down the street and she nodded at that last booth, still devoid of customers. "*If* there's going to be a senior prom."

Logan shifted uncomfortably, but didn't let himself follow Sue Ellen's gaze. "Of course there's going to be a senior prom. No matter what."

The hairdresser lifted a doubtful eyebrow, still looking at the booth that customarily raised all the necessary funds to lavishly decorate the high-school auditorium for the senior class's prom. Then she looked back at Logan, her expression speculative. "Maybe you could buy the first—"

"No way," he said hastily.

"C'mon." Her voice was coaxing. "We need to get some customers down there or everyone will be—"

"Talking about the fact that the money jar is empty, I know," Logan finished for her. "But why are you looking at me? Chris's daughter's the one who's hoping for a prom this year. Tell *him* to go over there and get the ball rolling."

Sue Ellen glanced around as if wary of being overheard, then leaned forward and whispered, "He's afraid of her."

Though unsurprised, Logan rolled his eyes. Three-fourths of the male population of Strawberry Bay was afraid of the woman volunteering in the senior prom booth, while the other quarter was afraid of what their wives or girlfriends would say if they approached her. "She's not that bad," he lied.

"It's a *kissing* booth, Logan!" Sue Ellen exclaimed. "I know she has a younger sister who's a high-school senior, but someone should have realized that that woman in that particular kind of booth might prove the end of a long-standing custom.''

Logan winced. Strawberry Bay, like any small town, was long on tradition and long on talk. Gossip would go on for decades that Elena O'Brien's year in the senior prom kissing booth was the first year in twenty that the enterprise flopped.

Still, he was *not* going over there. Knowing Elena, she was more than likely thrilled by her solitude.

Before he could change his mind, he bid goodbye to Sue Ellen and ducked between the massive angled panels set up for the art show. He didn't want to think about Elena and her predicament any longer. Out of sight, out of mind, he told himself.

Yet even from here he could feel her disturbing presence. A few months before, thanks to his brother's romance with Elena's best friend, Elena had vaulted back into his life. Though he hadn't seen her since his last days in high school, she'd instantly gone about disturbing his peace of mind, just as before.

Worse now, because the grown-up Elena was a puzzle, one minute an icy fortress, the next a hornet, buzzing loudly and ready to sting. The last time they'd been face-to-face was a couple of weekends ago, when she was maid of honor and he was best man at Griffin and Annie's wedding. He'd done his best to ignore her and the sexual vibration she started humming inside him too, because in recent weeks simplicity had become Logan's new watchword.

And nothing about Elena had ever been simple.

Pushing her out of his thoughts once more, Logan hurried around the corner of the first aisle, barrelling into Si Thomas, one of the men who used to work for him at Chase Electronics. They bounced apart and Logan saw that the other man's glasses were dangling over one ear, the wire stem bent.

"Lord, I'm sorry, Si. What can I do?"

The other man pulled his glasses off to inspect the damage. "No big deal. I'll just—" He stopped, then squinted up at Logan. "As a matter of fact, there *is* something you can do."

"Name it."

Si smiled. "My wife is on the high school's senior prom committee. She just begged me to find someone willing to..."

Logan didn't listen to the rest of the request. Hands over his ears, he desperately backed away, then dashed down the next aisle to lose himself amongst the other browsers. When Si didn't follow—thank God—Logan slowed his steps and glanced idly at the displayed artwork.

He paused as a painting caught his eye. It was a watercolor, he thought, but not in the bland pastels he usually associated with the medium. Whether its style was abstract or impressionist or something else altogether, he didn't know, but the painting was obviously of a woman lying in bed. The tousled, raspberry-colored covers only hinted at her form, but the pearly, bare shoulders and the full, rosy mouth were those of a young woman. The rest of her face was obscured by her arm flung over her eyes. Inky hair was spread across the pillow.

The painting intrigued and unsettled him with its juxtaposition of decadent bed and sleeping woman. It was almost as if she was waiting to be awakened by just the right man.

"Hey, Logan," a voice said.

Logan turned to greet the male half of a high-school-aged couple. "Hey, Tyler." Tyler Evans lived on the estate that bordered Logan's parents'. His father owned a produce distribution company—selling most of Strawberry Bay's strawberries—and his mother served on several charity boards with Logan's mother.

A petite, very pretty teenager with black hair and blue eyes stood beside the young man.

"This is Gabby," Tyler said, sliding a proprietary arm around her waist. "We met in art class."

The pretty young woman, who looked disturbingly familiar to Logan, smiled. He found himself smiling back. "Nice to meet you, Gabby."

Tyler hugged her closer to his side and kissed her hair in the way that young lovers do, as if he couldn't help himself. Gabby's cheeks went pink, but her smile deepened and Logan knew he had to be wrong in his first suspicion—that Gabby was related to his nemesis, Elena. Though their looks were similar, Gabby appeared warm and approachable, and she'd obviously enjoyed Tyler's affection. Touching Elena, however, was like grabbing a handful of stinging nettles.

"This is Logan Chase," Tyler told Gabby.

Her smile turned Mona Lisa-like. "I know. My sister has, um, pointed him out before."

"Ah." Logan nodded. So he'd been right after all. "Gabby *O'Brien*. Elena's sister."

"Hey! So you know Elena?" Tyler's voice turned heartily cheerful. "We were just going over to see her. Maybe you'd like to come along."

Logan blinked. "You think I'd like to *what?*"

Tyler must really have it bad for little Gabby, because his cheery expression didn't change. "Go see Elena. In the kissing booth. I'm going over there to—" he swallowed "—buy a kiss."

Logan knew he must have heard wrong. "You're going to *what?*"

Tyler gulped again, his face betraying its first signs of panic. "Buy a kiss," he said bravely.

Logan laughed. "Not and survive you're not. She'll stab a kid like you before she kisses you."

Gabby giggled and Logan looked at her, slightly ashamed for saying such a thing in front of the Frost Queen's sister. But hell, Gabby had to know it was true.

"Someone has to go over there and pay for a kiss," Tyler said stubbornly. "Once one man, uh, survives, more customers will come along. We need that money for the prom decorations."

"Kid…" Logan ran a hand through his hair, trying to think of how to explain the situation tactfully.

"Someone has to," Tyler insisted, looking young,

noble and not just a little bit stupid. "And I guess that someone has to be me."

Logan sighed. God. He'd tried, he really had. No one could say he hadn't. He sighed again.

"Never mind, kid." Logan inhaled a long, deep breath and wondered if the dread starting to build in his belly was what human sacrifices had felt on their way to execution. "I'll do it."

From fifty feet away, Logan gazed at the woman in the senior prom booth. If she wasn't so staggeringly beautiful, he thought, kissing her wouldn't be so bad.

Her midnight-black hair was sleek and shiny, hanging straight to her clean jawline and emphasizing her full, bewitching lips. Her skin, fine-pored and unmarked by even a single freckle, was a golden cream color that made her black-lashed blue eyes stand out like sapphires.

If that wasn't enough to mess with a man's brain, ever since she was sixteen years old, Elena O'Brien had possessed the kind of curves that made men from 12 to 112 stop, stare then salivate.

The hell of it was, Elena had a beautiful face paired with one hot, bodacious bod. It was the kind of coupling that made a man think only of...well, coupling. But Logan knew from personal experience that it wasn't wise to let your wits wander southward when you were around Elena. While you were busy dreaming of her scratching your back, she'd be busy finding ways to scratch your eyes out.

The funny thing was, people genuinely liked her as a person. Women included, despite the kind of loveliness that might inspire jealousy. She was reputed to be an indefatigable employee and Logan's new sister-in-law swore she was a terrific friend. But when a man approached Elena O'Brien as a man, she'd hiss and spit and scare the poor guy off. Sometimes off women altogether.

Rumor had it there was a guy in the next city who, after one date with Elena, had moved back in with his mother and was now raising bunny rabbits.

Inhaling a fortifying breath, Logan began strolling toward the kissing booth. As if sensing his destination, the people in front of him parted, clearing his path just the way the citizens of Dodge City cleared a path for the white-hatted sheriff in a bad Western.

He shoved his hands in the pockets of his worn jeans and ignored the chug of his blood pulsing through his veins. He hoped like hell his face was expressionless. Conventional wisdom said it wasn't smart to show fear around animals that bite.

The senior prom committee's booth was situated in the shade of mature trees and had a fanciful, castle-like facade that was painted white and decorated with bright pink and red tissue-paper flowers. The colors framed Elena's vibrant beauty perfectly, and as Logan approached she raised her black brows in twin arches just as perfect.

He shoved his hands deeper in his pockets and curved his lips in what he hoped appeared a relaxed, casual smile. "Hey, there," he said, bracing for the expected verbal lashing.

An overlarge, empty glass fishbowl sat on the booth's narrow countertop. It was where the kiss money was supposed to go, and in other years the thing had overflowed with bills. Elena didn't spare it a glance as she slowly slid from a high stool to land on the soles of her sneakers. "What do you want?" she asked, her tone on the low end of the truculence scale.

Well, good. Apparently she didn't immediately assume he was after a kiss, which would be sure to set her hackles rising. "I, um, just thought I'd say hi."

"Yeah?" As usual, she wasn't much impressed with him. "Hi." Her gaze fell to the toes of her shoes.

Something about the short response put Logan on alert. The truth was, he'd accidentally and unfortunately stood her up two weeks ago, the night of the wedding rehearsal dinner. Given their past history and the daggers she'd thrown with her eyes all the way down the church aisle, he'd been convinced she'd take this opportunity to launch a full-on verbal assault.

"Is something wrong?" he asked warily.

Instead of answering, she flushed.

Logan's jaw dropped. With her gaze still on her feet, he could only see the top of her head and the red color crawling up her neck. He didn't know what to think. She was never subdued, shy or, for that matter, even civil around him. "Are you sick?" he asked.

Her head jerked up. "Is that what they're saying?"

She sounded hopeful, Logan thought, still trying to comprehend her out-of-character reserve.

"Is that it?" she insisted, that hopeful note intensifying. "Does everyone think I'm contagious or something?"

He couldn't lie to her. "No," he answered, stepping forward. "But, uh, Elena…"

"Never mind." She scuttled back against the stool. "I didn't really think so." As if to prove she was in her usual fine fettle, she lifted her chin to half glower at him.

Still puzzled, Logan studied her face. There was definitely a flush on her skin, and he was certain it wasn't a fever or even a flush of ill temper. *Hell.* It couldn't be, it wasn't possible, was it? Was Elena truly bothered by her lack of business?

Damn it, that wouldn't make things any easier. He'd come over here to help out the senior prom fund. To save noble knight Tyler from Elena's wrath, and possibly a career in the rabbit industry. She'd murder Logan if she somehow leaped to the conclusion he was here to buy a kiss to save her from humiliation.

But Elena *humiliated?* It just didn't seem possible.

Not sure what to believe, he decided to postpone immediate action by smiling again, trying once more to appear friendly. "Have you heard from Griffin and Annie?" The two were on their honeymoon, touring Europe.

"Yeah," she said softly. "A postcard from

France.'' The corners of her mouth lifted in a sweet, genuine smile.

Uh-oh. At the sight of that enchanting smile, Logan felt his knees go weak. His brain stuttered as whatever amount of blood supposed to keep the top half of his body in working order instantly rushed lower.

Her eyes narrowed and her body stiffened. ''What's wrong with you?'' she demanded.

He sucked in a quick, desperate breath. ''N-nothing.'' With another breath, his voice got stronger. ''Not a thing.''

She relaxed slightly, though her eyes remained watchful. ''Okay.''

Whew. That was a close one. A really close one. Elena hated when a man displayed a reaction to her beauty. Particularly when *he* did. But it was an impossibly difficult thing to control so instead he just took great pains to hide it.

With a show of nonchalance, he stepped closer and leaned casually against the side of the booth. ''I met your sister.''

Her face brightened, that smile threatening to blossom again. God, she was gorgeous.

''You met Gabby? She's here?''

Logan nodded. ''With Tyler Evans, who I'm guessing is her boyfriend.''

Elena shrugged. ''I suppose. One of those casual things, though. Gabby's going to UC Berkeley in the fall.'' Her voice filled with pride. ''Pre-med.''

Impressed, Logan raised his eyebrows. ''Tyler just told me she's an artist too.''

"Mm. A hobby." She raised her shoulders in a little shrug. "But it's her brains that will take her farthest."

Her dismissal of Gabby's other talents rankled Logan. "Yes, but—" He bit back the words, thinking better of exposing his personal raw spots. "I'm sure she'll be a success at whatever she chooses."

"That's right," Elena replied. "Gabby's going to have everything. Perfect prom, perfect graduation—"

"Perfect pre-med college life," he finished for her wryly.

She apparently hadn't caught his tone because for once she smiled as if she really liked him. "Exactly. That's what we've been working for."

We? That earlier rankle edged into a strange worry. "Elena…"

"Hmm?" she said absently, her gaze drifting over his shoulder.

Logan turned, saw a man walking toward the kissing booth, then saw the man suddenly recognize the woman on the other side of the counter. The man abruptly spun about, and hastily got in line at the booth supporting the local children's hospital, as if that was his chosen destination all the while.

"Well," Logan said with a laugh. "It should be interesting to see how they do a Caribbean thread-wrap on that guy's hair." The man was completely bald.

When she didn't answer, he swung around. Her eyes appeared so blue their color hit him like a blow, and he suddenly realized there were tears in them. He swallowed, feeling almost sick. "Elena—"

"Don't. Don't say anything." Her voice was tight. "I'm in this dumb booth for Gabby. *I* don't care, do you understand?"

Even though her eyes were watery, she could still pin him painfully with her glare. "And if you try to tell anybody, *anybody* I was crying over something as stupid as that man not wanting to buy a kiss from me, I'll…I'll…"

It was testament to how truly upset she was that she couldn't complete her threat. "Boil my toes?" he offered helpfully, trying to give her a chance to recover. "Stick ants in my ears?"

That got her. "Ants in your ears?" She flicked one fallen tear away with her thumb. "Oh, just be quiet."

"Elena—"

"Leave it alone, will you?" She'd blinked away the last of the tears, but her customary prickly armor wasn't yet quite back in place.

"I'm sorr—"

"I *told* you. Leave it alone. My mood has nothing to do with the kissing booth. I'm just having a bad day." She glared at him again. "Can't I have a bad day?"

Since she generally *caused* bad days—his—he was unsure how to answer. "What's wrong?" he asked quietly.

"Everything," she muttered, looking away. "You name it."

Logan's blood chilled. Something *was* wrong.

Could it be man trouble? He hadn't heard she was seeing anyone, and God knew it would take a special kind of man to knock that boulder-size chip off her shoulder, but…. But it made him damn angry to think someone could have gotten to her heart, then broken it. "Is it a man?" he asked.

"Of course not," she answered, but still, she didn't sound like herself and she didn't meet his eyes.

"Who the hell is he?" Logan demanded.

She shot him a startled, sidelong look, then shook her head. "No, no. It isn't like that."

Not good enough. He still didn't feel relieved. "What exactly is it like then?" he pressed.

That got her bristling again. "Logan—"

"What's the trouble?" he said through his teeth, his anger unexpectedly jumping to match hers. "Tell me *now*."

"Oh, fine!" Her gaze slammed into his. "If you really want to know, I'll admit it. The trouble *is* this." Her hand flew wildly in the direction of the empty fishbowl, and she made contact, sending it rocking. "It's mortifying, okay?"

Ah. Well. Logan felt his surprising, unfamiliar surge of anger instantly subside into something quite different. Not that her words were anything to get all worked up about. Except that Elena O'Brien, the toughest, prickliest, least-likely-to-surrender woman he knew, had just admitted out loud she actually possessed normal, human feelings.

Suddenly the prospect of kissing her didn't seem quite so dreadful after all.

He ran his tongue over his teeth, then smiled. It felt like a charming smile. "Hmm. Well. I may not be able to do a lot of things, but I *can* do something about—" he gestured toward the fishbowl "—that."

Her eyes widened, then narrowed, her mouth bunching up. She could have been sucking on a lemon. "Don't you dare!"

It occurred to him he should possibly be insulted by her apparent distaste. "What's wrong now?" he said grumpily, hoping like hell she wasn't going to be thorny about this.

"Logan." Angry heat flared in her eyes. "Don't you dare think about kissing me."

Damn her. She *was* going to be thorny about this, and here he was, about to do her a favor.

Then her eyes narrowed even more. "Oh, I get it now. You think you're doing me a favor, don't you?"

While he tried to look properly wounded by her correct guess, she propped her hands on her hips and stomped closer to the counter. "Listen, Logan. I don't need your pity."

She was close enough that he could detect her scent. She wore an exotic fragrance that smelled like flowers heated by the sun. Logan tried thinking of some response to what she'd just said, but his head was suddenly spinning again.

She could tell that too. Her eyes rolled. "Uh!" She spun away.

He reached out, grabbed her wrist.

Elena froze. A tremor ran down her back then her head turned slowly toward him. She looked at his hand on her, then looked at his face. "Let go of me," she said.

"No," he answered. Her arm was quivering against his hand and Logan didn't know if it was outrage or embarrassment or some combination of both. He hauled her closer, so that only the narrow wooden counter separated them.

Her breath was coming so hard and so fast that her astounding breasts were heaving against the cotton of her shirt. Staring at the sight, his brain whirled again and she almost used his distraction to pull away, but then some instinct deeper than lust made his hold tighten possessively.

"I don't want your pity," she said again.

"Pity," he repeated. "You don't know how much I wish I was going to do this out of pity." He crowded closer to the counter, getting closer to her.

That flush was running up her neck again, past her mouth, over her cheeks. Her chin lifted. "Why is it then?" she hissed. "Don't tell me. I can guess. It's—"

"Don't." It was his turn to say the word. "You're in the kissing booth and I'm buying one kiss. Hell, Elena. Let's just leave it at that."

He bent his head. He hadn't kissed her in eleven years, since she was sixteen and he was eighteen. He hesitated now, because the memory of those kisses wasn't something he was quite ready to relinquish. The reality of kissing Elena couldn't be as good as he remembered.

Her body was trembling again and her eyes were

snapping blue fire, but she wasn't trying to get away and he knew he couldn't get away with retreating from this kiss. Hell, it had been leading to this for the past few months, ever since they had met again. It was probably plain good sense to get it over with.

He covered her lips with his.

She inhaled sharply at the contact and he froze. Her body shook, and he dropped her wrist to cup her shoulders with his palms. He slid his tongue between her lips. Not into her mouth, just between her soft, full, how-could-he-have-forgotten-their-decadent-taste? lips.

She inhaled sharply again, unwittingly drawing in his tongue, and Logan's senses, instead of whirling like the dervishes he expected, heightened. Focused.

From her throat came the tiniest of moans, the sound vibrating against his tongue. Her flower-scent bloomed around them and he tasted her desire in the heat of her mouth and in the way her tongue slid against his, as if she had to know its texture, too.

All his muscles tensed, every one, everywhere, going rock-solid. He pressed her mouth harder, took the kiss deeper, and even though he felt his blood rush through his body and his heartbeat jump to unprecedented speed, his mind remained crystal-clear, as if to sear this new kiss in his memory.

His eyes opened, and he saw hers as languid slits of blue, like pieces of hot summer sky. He saw it all in them: the attraction, the arousal and then he saw something else.

Vulnerability.

Oh, hell.

Blood pounding and every nerve howling in protest, Logan broke the kiss, slowly but surely easing Elena away. He knew she was staring at him, but he refused to meet her eyes. Instead, he concentrated on getting his breathing back to normal, while one hand slid into his pocket.

Just that morning he'd met a friend and traded his Beemer for a well-worn pickup and some big-billed cash. He pulled the wad of bills out now and looked at them, the numbers on the corners making as little sense to him as the advanced calculus formulas had in college. Blinking, he focused harder, found the one he wanted, pulled it free.

Still without looking at her, he dropped it in the fishbowl. Grover Cleveland's face fluttered to the bottom.

He turned to go.

"Wait."

Reluctantly he swung back and looked at Elena. She was completely recovered, he was relieved to see, except for the slightly swollen appearance of her lips. Her blue eyes were back to their usual cool and the one brow she raised was just as confident and saucy as always.

"The senior prom committee thanks you," she said.

Logan released a silent sigh, immediately understanding the remark's significance. It wasn't Elena who thanked him, but the prom committee. Whew. He nodded, and found he was recovered enough himself to touch his forehead in a casual, two-fingered salute.

He turned and ambled away, feeling as if he'd just dodged a deadly bullet. Some sixth sense had warned him against letting that kiss go any further. He knew that if he'd made Elena helpless in his arms, she would never have forgiven him. And he knew he would never have been able to forget Elena.

Chapter Two

Her shift in the kissing booth over, Elena O'Brien pushed through the crowd in the direction she'd seen Logan take after he'd left her. Her fingers touched the folded bill stuffed in her pocket. It was the only thing that kept her going after him.

She'd rather be running in the opposite direction.

There was only one man who could make her feel adolescent-awkward. Only one man who could make her feel a half-shy, half-wild sixteen again, her shoes sliding off her heels because her *abuela*—grandmother—always bought them big for a growing girl. At sixteen she remembered her lips throbbing too, scrubbed clean at Nana's insistence of the scarlet lipstick Elena wanted so badly to wear.

Only girls that were *payo*—trashy—painted their

mouths. Girls who did such a thing—and in such a color!—got the wrong kind of attention from boys.

Her *abuela,* God rest her soul, had been right about that.

Now, all these years later, Elena didn't have time for men and any kind of attention they might give her. Not when there was Gabby to think of and all the money that it would require to put her through college and then medical school. Elena was working two jobs already and, she thought with a sigh, she might have to pick up a third to pay for the damage the recent earthquake had done to the home she and Gabby had inherited from their grandmother.

Anyway, the truth was that Elena had lousy luck when it came to men. It wasn't much hardship to sacrifice them so that her sister could achieve their dream.

Catching sight of broad shoulders and a dark golden head amongst those gathering around a small stage on her right, Elena's feet paused of their own accord, her heart twitching in that stupid, childish way again. Despite the fact that Logan Chase was her best friend's brother-in-law, she gave serious second thoughts to letting him live with his own mistake. She didn't want another confrontation with him.

But she steeled her spine and headed his way, because she refused to be ruled by her ridiculous reactions to him. Pride demanded it. Anyway, he was never going to know how he affected her. She wouldn't give him the satisfaction.

She excused herself through the knot of people until she stood directly behind him. "Logan." When he didn't immediately turn, she touched his back.

Something jolted through her fingers, shooting up her arm. Logan jerked around.

"You," he said, his brown eyes wide.

Elena stared. The word had briefly formed his mouth into a kiss and her lips started throbbing again. Not because he made her recall those lipstick scrubbings as she'd tried to tell herself before, but because not twenty minutes ago he'd pressed that mouth against hers. The kiss had spun her away from the kissing booth, from Strawberry Bay, even—unbelievably—from her worries and responsibilities.

Biting down on her betraying bottom lip, she shoved her hands in her pockets. The bill crackled against her fingers, reminding her she'd had a purpose beyond reliving that kiss to seek him out.

"You made a mistake," she said, drawing out the thousand-dollar bill.

He glanced at the money, then back at her face. "Who's in the kissing booth?"

Willing herself not to flush, she pretended she hadn't admitted to him that her failure in the booth bothered her. "I took the first shift because everyone else had a conflict. This is the Homecoming Queen's hour."

"Ah." His very white smile broke across his face, carving lines into his lean, tanned cheeks. "Good."

Elena stiffened. "Yes, well, I'm sure she'll have much better success."

"Damn it, Elena." Logan's smile died and he

pushed his dark gold hair behind his ears. It was longer than she'd ever seen it, almost messy, and it fell forward again immediately. He pushed at it once more, an awkward movement, as if he didn't know how to manage the new length. "I didn't mean that the way it sounds."

"How did you mean it then?" Oh, she was proud of herself for how cool she sounded. Almost uncaring.

He muttered something under his breath. "I—"

The rest of his words were cut off by a trumpet fanfare from the speakers set up nearby. Almost immediately a line of teeny tiny girls in pink tights, leotards, and tap shoes shuffle-stepped onto the stage. The line leader carried a sign proclaiming them to be Miss Bunny's Tapping Tots. Applause erupted from the crowd around them.

Logan said something to her, but it was lost in the first notes of "The Good Ship Lollipop." Elena shook her head and pointed at her ears to indicate she couldn't hear, bringing her attention back to the bill in her hand.

She held it mutely up to him.

He shook his head.

She shook it in his face. "A mistake," she mouthed.

When he didn't respond, she gritted her teeth and grabbed his arm to tow him somewhere quiet. She was due at her second job in less than an hour.

The art show was set up a little ways from the stage, and the panels on which the paintings were hung muffled most of the music. Elena halted in the first aisle and faced Logan. "This is your money," she said, holding out the bill. When he'd dropped it in the bowl, she hadn't immediately noticed its denomination because she'd been distracted—okay, fine, *dazzled*—by their kiss.

A small smile playing over his wide mouth, he pushed his hands in the pockets of his jeans, looking down on her. He was a rangy six-one or six-two, much taller than her five-feet-and-almost-five-inches. Maybe that was why he always managed to make her feel like she was on her first date.

Or maybe that was because he had *been* her first date.

"That's the kissing booth's money," Logan said.

She frowned at him. "Do you need glasses or something? This is a thousand-dollar bill!"

He shrugged. "You don't think you're worth it?"

She swallowed a sound of annoyance. This is what he did to her. He either made her feel clumsy, cross or a lethal combination of the two that played havoc with her self-control. "Logan."

"Hmm?"

"It's no big deal." Her voice was even, reasonable. Very mature. "You accidentally put the wrong bill into the jar. Give me five bucks, I'll give you this back, and we'll be fine."

He laughed. "We haven't been fine since—"

"Since my best friend started going out with your brother." Her path and Logan's hadn't crossed for years, but then Annie and Griffin had fallen in love.

"I was going to say we haven't been fine since the night we met."

In an instant, Elena's mouth dried. She'd been newly sixteen, newly orphaned, new to town. He'd been eighteen, golden, a man in her eyes. Her heart jumped around in her chest just as it had done then and she felt the flush of sexual arousal bloom over her skin, just as it had done then too. He'd awakened her that night.

Then a week later humiliated her.

Her fingers tightened on the crisp paper and she looked down at it, then back up to his face. "What game are you playing?" she said slowly.

Now it was his turn to look annoyed. "What the hell do you mean by that?"

Her eyes narrowed. "Why would you put this much money in the fishbowl?"

He opened his mouth. Closed it. His hand lifted. Fell to his side in a fist. "You are too much work," he finally ground out. "Can't you just accept it as a donation?"

A thousand dollars for a kiss? A thousand-dollar donation for *prom decorations?* Her face felt stiff and she remembered all over again that Logan's family owned Chase Electronics, the biggest employer in town. He'd grown up within the walls of an estate that was on California's historic register.

"Pardon me for not understanding how little this is to the privileged set," she said. "On my side of town a thousand dollars is a lot of money."

"Elena, I didn't mean it like that." He shook his head, sighing. It sounded like frustration. "Would you believe me if I told you I wish it wasn't always like this between us?"

It was on the tip of her tongue to ask him how he wished it *was* between them. But that was dangerous, much too much like *truly* wishing, and though Logan had once upon a time awakened her with a kiss—kisses—she'd given up on princes and happy-ever-afters long ago.

Over his shoulder she spotted her sister with Tyler Evans, turning the corner to the next aisle. Elena frowned, her constant niggle of worry over Gabby growing as she caught sight of the teenagers' entwined hands.

"Fine then," she told Logan, shoving the thousand-dollar bill back into her pocket. "I'll make sure your money gets to the committee." Without waiting for his response, she trailed behind Gabby and Tyler.

Logan trailed her.

She turned her head to look at him. "Why are you following me?"

"Because, damn it, I'm never satisfied with the way things end between us."

There was something hot in his eyes. She hated when he did that. At will, it seemed, he could put a sexual burn into his gaze. She was sure he did it to fluster her, so of course she'd die before she'd let him know that look made her knees quiver and her stomach flutter.

"Stop doing that." She made sure she sounded irritated.

He shook his head, then put his hand on her arm, halting her movement. "Elena…"

Her body was trembling, it was horribly embarrassing, but it was. She tensed her muscles, hoping he wouldn't detect her helpless reaction to his touch. What an unsophisticate he'd consider her if he knew.

"Elena." His voice softened, hoarsened. That heat in his brown eyes was melting the strength she counted on for survival. "You are so madden—"

"Elena! Someone bought my painting!"

At the sound of her sister's voice, Elena found the will to pull away from the spell of Logan's gaze and touch. She turned to face the approaching Gabby, Tyler a bit behind her. "What, Gabriellita?"

Gabby's face was flushed and her eyes sparkled. "I sold my very first painting!"

Elena tried to catch up to her sister's excitement. "You brought your art to the show." She vaguely remembered Gabby telling her that she and Tyler were each submitting a painting, but the details had gotten lost in all the other details of their busy life.

Gabby nodded. "Mr. Barger—he's the one in charge of the art show—said it sold about ten minutes ago. And Mrs. Eddleston from the bank is writing a check for Tyler's painting right now."

Her little sister looked as though she was about to pop, and it made Elena grin.

"Congratulations, Gabby." It was Logan.

Gabby's head jerked up and she blinked, as if noticing him for the first time. Hot color rushed across her face. "Thank you. Really. Thank you."

Confused, Elena looked between Gabby and Logan. "What's going on?"

"I bought the painting," Logan said, his gaze on Gabby. "You can verify it with Mr. Barger, by the way, that I didn't realize who the artist was until after the sale."

Elena turned to look at him, still bewildered. "You bought a painting?"

There was a funny expression on Logan's face. "I've just moved and I could use something for my walls. The painting..." He cleared his throat, shrugged, looked away. "Called to me."

There was a buzzing in Elena's ears. "Wh—" She had to stop, start again. "Which painting, exactly, did you show today, Gabby?"

Her sister gulped. Audibly.

"No," Elena protested, her voice swallowed up by horror.

Gabby nodded, an expression somewhere between mischief and apology in her eyes. *"Elena in Bed."*

Elena's gaze flew to Logan, even as a flush moved just as quickly from her toes to her forehead. Forget worrying about looking sixteen. Because now the man had bought the right to look at her—all day and all night if he wanted.

And though she appeared decent enough in the painting, it didn't help her state of mind to know—and Logan likely suspected—that beneath those covers she'd been stark naked.

* * *

Late Sunday afternoon, Logan blasted U2 through his stereo speakers as inspiration while he stripped the fourteen coats of paint covering the banister of the stairway in his three-story Victorian. His fingers ached from his grip on the scraper, his back would never be the same after spending the day half-bent, and he was stooping because his knees were already bruised to hell and back. But he'd never been happier in his life, he thought, singing along with Bono. Yeah, man. It *was* a beautiful day.

It took a while for a muffled banging to distinguish itself from the drumline of the song. Someone was knocking on his front door.

Logan descended the steps at a jog, then paused to turn down the stereo before approaching the foyer. With his hand on the doorknob, he hesitated. Maybe he should—

No, even if it *was* good ol' Jonathon Chase, his father, intent on another turn of the guilt screws, it was too late to pretend he wasn't home. Bracing himself, he pulled open the door.

Elena stood on the other side, looking as surprised to see him as he was to see her. They stared at each other for a moment, then she blinked, her gaze traveling down, then back up to meet his.

"You're, um, dirty," she pointed out, her voice as surprised as her expression.

He nodded, his own gaze involuntarily zeroing in on her full mouth. Dirty in his mind too, he could have added, because he'd been dwelling on that kiss they'd shared. Not to mention all the time he'd spent studying his new art acquisition, *Elena in Bed.*

Uh-oh. He suddenly had a very good idea about why the beautiful bane of his life was standing on his doorstep. She'd made some vague threats before hurrying off the day before about getting the painting back.

No, he resolved instantly. No way. It was his! It felt damn good to have something she wanted for once. What other man could say that?

"May I come in?" she asked.

Oh, she wanted the painting bad, Logan decided, because she was actually managing to sound sort of friendly.

Which immediately edged up the dial on his Trouble Meter. It was best not to let her inside. Call it a premonition, call it learning from past mistakes, but he and Elena did not do well in close proximity. Consider that kiss. No, better not. Not when she was so near.

He stepped out onto the porch, trying to invent a polite refusal. *Hustle her toward home.* Out of his life, good. Without his painting. Very good.

But now, a few steps closer to her and with his initial surprise out of the way, his eyes widened again. Elena appeared exhausted. Strangely defenseless too, with her sumptuous curves swallowed up by a white T-shirt and a baggy pair of denim overalls.

With a pale face and tired shadows beneath her baby blues, she was also so gut-wrenchingly gorgeous it made a man want to slay her dragons as much as he wanted to seduce her. Cursing his own weakness, he found himself turning right around to usher her inside.

"Is everything okay?" he asked, directing her toward the front room. Layers of wallpaper were peeled back from the plaster in long curls. Pink stripes over yellow flowers over a design that might once have been green but was now grayish.

She paused in the middle of the room, taking in the bay window, the wallpaper curls, the two old recliners—one with duct tape on the seat—that faced a big-screen TV sitting on a platform of cinder block and plywood. He watched TV sometimes while he worked. The recliners had been left behind by the previous homeowner.

She looked over at him, her expression amazed. "You *do* actually live here. Your mother gave me this address when I called but I wasn't sure I understood her correctly."

Logan gestured toward the recliner sans duct tape, and then frowned as he watched her drop to the seat with a little sigh. She seemed glad to have something beneath her.

"Oh, Mom has the story straight," he replied, scrutinizing Elena even more closely. "Can I get you something to eat? A beer? Soda?"

She waved a weary hand. "Whatever."

When he came back in with two bottles of beer in one hand and a plate of cold pizza in the other, Elena was collapsed against the back cushion of her chair. He handed her a bottle and put the pizza on the scarred end table between the two recliners, nudging over the remote control to make room.

She took a long swallow of beer then cast him a look. "You really quit Chase Electronics?"

He took a chug from his own bottle. "Yep."

"You moved out of your condo and bought this Victorian. On *my* side of town."

"Yep. Though the condo is actually Griffin's. He and Annie will live in it when they get back from the honeymoon. Until they find their own house, anyway."

"You quit Chase Electronics," Elena repeated as if still not quite believing it, then took a longer swallow from her bottle.

"And I bought my buddy Reuben's rehab business—which doesn't mean much more than his tools and this house which he was only half finished converting into apartments. But he wanted to move to Oregon with his girlfriend and I wanted to break the chains tying me to my desk at Chase Electronics. A match made in heaven."

"You know how to do all this?" She gestured with her beer toward the wallpaper and then the bay windows. Half the trimwork around them was missing, the other half was shedding paint coat number fifteen.

He shrugged. "We'll find out."

Her jaw dropped.

He laughed. "It's not as reckless as it sounds. Though I got my MBA at Stanford, I have an undergraduate degree in Industrial Arts. I've always wanted to work with my hands."

It had been his brother almost passing up on love and his parents celebrating forty years of a merger instead of a marriage, to wake Logan up to that fact. He'd opened his eyes to find himself tied to a dreary job in the family company and also tied to an almost-fiancé. Both fulfilled other people's expectations—but didn't do a thing for him.

Elena drank from her beer again. "Your father…"

"Is predicting disaster. Me on my knees begging for my old position back at Chase Electronics."

"You look determined to prove him wrong."

"Yeah." Logan had overcomplicated his life for years by going along with dear old dad, but it was simple now. He'd focus solely on building his business—a business that would satisfy *him*. "People are interested in restoring the Victorians and California bungalows around town—even more so since last summer's earthquake damaged several of them."

At the mention of the earthquake, she frowned and then quickly drained her beer and carefully set the bottle on the floor. "Well, I'm sure both of us have better things to do. I came to pick up my painting."

He lifted an eyebrow. "You mean *my* painting?"

Her lips compressed in annoyance. "I'm paying you for it," she said, patting the pants pocket of her overalls.

"I never said I'd sell it."

"*Logan.* I didn't have time for this yesterday, I had to get to work. But there's no point in arguing. I have the money." Her hand went to her pocket again as she jumped to her feet. Then she swayed, looking dizzy.

Logan rose in concern as she put an unsteady hand on the back of her chair. "Elena?"

She blinked at him. "I'm fine," she said quickly. "I just stood up too fast."

He took a step toward her anyway.

Thank God. It gave him enough time to catch her as she fell.

He figured she was fainting. Or maybe she was passing out from a combination of no food and that one beer. Either way, he expected she'd keep her mouth shut.

But cradled in his arms as he climbed the stairs toward his second-floor apartment, Elena gave him grief.

"Put me down. I'm fine. Just a little tired or something. Put me down. Let go. I stood up too fast. I'm fine. Put me *down*."

He let her drone on, which she did, of course, until he dropped her onto the mattress in his bedroom. Then he told her to shut up.

Unnecessary, though. Because her mouth had snapped closed, mid complaint, when she saw what he'd hung on the wall opposite his bed.

Damn.

Her gaze moved to him accusingly and she struggled to her elbows. "You told me yesterday that you wouldn't hang it! You promised."

He shook his head. "I promised I wouldn't let anyone see it. But enough about that. You need to lie back and rest.''

"I need to get my painting back!"

Double damn.

He sighed. "It's my painting, darling. And you're not going anywhere until we figure out why you went down for the count. Should I call a doctor?''

"Of course not." She sat up.

His hand on her shoulder, he forced her back to the pillows. "Did you eat today?"

She looked ready to take a bite out of *him*. "I assisted at the cooking school this morning. We made seven-grain waffles with strawberry syrup. I'm sure I took a taste."

A *taste*. "And then what?" he asked.

"And then I spent a few hours wading through the summer admission applications stacking up in my office, if that's any of your business."

Though officially an "administrative assistant," Logan had heard she virtually ran the admissions office at the local community college single-handedly. He shook his head. "Elena, it's Sunday. You worked two jobs today and you went to work yesterday as well. No wonder you're dead on your feet."

She glared at him. "Some of us can't afford to sneer at overtime." One hand slid into her pocket and the other grabbed his. Paper slapped against his palm. "There. Your money."

Instead of green bills, he looked down at a section of the newspaper folded into a small rectangle. "What's this?"

She made a little huff of irritation and fished through her other pocket. "A mistake." She drew out a wad of cash. "Here."

He avoided accepting it by unfolding the newspaper to glance at the circled ads. "You're moving?"

"Temporarily. If I can find something we can afford for a month or two."

"Why?" He looked at her over the top of the newspaper.

She sighed. "They did another round of earthquake inspections in my area and guess what? They found serious damage to our foundation. Gabby and I have to be out while it's being repaired."

"No earthquake insurance?"

Her blue eyes tried to wither him. "I don't own any diamond mines either," she said, then swung her legs over the bed to sit up.

She had to flatten her free hand to the mattress to steady herself and her face seemed to go paler.

That sign of vulnerability made *him* feel a little sick. "Are you having any luck finding someplace to live?"

She took a fortifying breath. "On my budget? Not yet. But I have a few other places to check out today."

"*Today?* Hell, Elena, you don't even have the strength to stand up."

She didn't protest, but she didn't agree either. Instead, she mutely held out the wad of cash.

He hesitated, mulling something over in his mind. If he made the offer, certainly she'd refuse. But hey, that was smart, he thought, because just the offer alone would earn him Good Guy points. In the game of Elena vs. Logan, nobody knew better than he that he needed all he could get.

She flopped the cash at him, both the bills and the gesture tired-looking. That did it. Witnessing yet another crack in that tough shell of hers made his stomach roll over and his last shred of self-preservation play dead.

"I'll give you the painting back on one condition," he said. "That you and Gabby move in here with me."

Her eyes widened. Oh yeah, Logan thought with great relief, she was gonna say no. And he was gonna get to keep *Elena in Bed* where she belonged.

Chapter Three

"I really had no choice, Gabby," Elena said a week later, avoiding her sister's eyes as she shoved another duffel bag into the already stuffed trunk of her car.

"I didn't say anything," Gabby answered, her voice threaded with a hint of laughter.

"No, but I can hear what you're thinking," Elena replied grumpily, then slammed the lid of the trunk with more ferocity than necessary. "Believe me, if there was another option we wouldn't be moving in with Logan."

Gabby didn't answer. Elena turned to watch her sister slide more boxes into the back seat of their old four-door sedan. Her graceful movements and the sweet expression on Gabby's face distracted Elena from her bad mood.

Her younger sister was precious to her, she thought in a sudden rush. Gabby summed up all the best qualities of the women in their family. She was beautiful, like their mother, but also full of Nana's good sense. And, like Elena, she didn't shrink from hard work.

Her sister had managed to avoid their flaws though, thank God. Their mother, Luisa, had carried an air of resigned sadness from the moment her husband had left her until the day she died. Nana hadn't wanted much from life, but that meant she expected too little too—both for herself and the two granddaughters she'd taken into her home after their mother's death. Marriage, babies, a man to provide, that was what their grandmother had told them to want, over and over again. She'd never considered that her granddaughters might desire something different for themselves.

She'd never considered that Elena had learned, in a few painful lessons, that it was foolish to depend on a man for anything.

As Gabby turned to take another box from her boyfriend Tyler, the sweet smile she gave him made clear she was much more trusting than Elena. It was one of two of Gabby's traits that made Elena uneasy.

"You're sure my art supplies are in your car?" Gabby asked Tyler.

That was the other.

Elena worried that her sister's preoccupation with her hobby of sketching and painting might affect their long-term goal—Gabby's medical degree. "You don't need to worry about your college information either," she told Gabby. "It's in the bright-blue accordion file, right there between the front seats. We won't lose sight of that."

"No," her sister replied, sending Tyler a pained look.

A look Elena decided to ignore. "I guess that's all we can fit for our first trip. When we come back we'll figure out some way to strap the futons and the table on the roof." Making a mental note to find some rope, she circled the car and pulled open the driver's side door.

"I'll ride with Tyler," Gabby said.

Elena frowned, worry niggling at her again. It wasn't that she begrudged her sister time with her boyfriend, but shouldn't they be weaning themselves from all this companionship? They would be heading off to separate colleges in a few months, after all— Gabby hours away at Berkeley and Tyler at the prestigious art school thirty minutes south of Strawberry Bay.

"All right," she finally agreed, with a little sigh. "But listen, both of you, no bothering Logan when we get to the house, okay?"

Gabby looked as if she was holding back a smile. "I don't think Tyler and I are the ones who bother him."

Elena made a face at her. "Ha ha. What I mean is…I don't want him, um, *involved* with us, you understand?"

Gabby shook her head. "Elena, we're going to be

living at the man's house for goodness sake. How are we going to manage to keep ourselves uninvolved?''

''We're staying in a separate apartment in his house. There are two on the second floor. One is his, one is ours.'' She looked down at the keys in her hand, trying to make clear—if just in her own mind— how she wanted this co-habitation to proceed. ''We're there not as family of course, not even as friends, but purely on a business basis.''

''I thought we were getting the apartment for free.'' Tyler spoke up for the first time. ''Sounds pretty friendly to me.''

Elena glared at them both. ''We have a bargain. You're right, no money is changing hands, but it's still strictly business.''

Gabby giggled and then stage-whispered to Tyler, ''She's letting him keep *Elena in Bed*.''

An embarrassed heat crawled up Elena's neck. ''It seemed sensible, Gabby. We need every penny we can save.''

Gabby shared a laughing look with Tyler. ''Oh yeah, big sister. Very sensible. Very uninvolving.''

Instead of defending herself, Elena jumped in the car and drove off. *Brats*. But she found herself smiling as she glimpsed the two of them in her rearview mirror, following in Tyler's fancy SUV. Despite their smart mouths, they did make an adorable couple, Gabby's exotic looks a foil for Tyler's blond all-American handsomeness.

And he did adore her sister. Though their breakup was inevitable, she didn't think he would hurt Gabby in the same way that Elena herself had been hurt by boys like him. The way their mother had been hurt by their father.

It took less than five minutes to reach Logan's large but run-down Victorian. It still surprised her, even though a week had gone by since her first visit, that he'd quit his job as a vice president of the Chase family company. And it surprised her even more that he'd left the posh side of town to live in this blue-collar neighborhood.

The homes here were a mix of old Victorians and bungalows, along with newer, modest dwellings and apartment buildings. It wasn't that the area was seedy, or even particularly neglected, but the people in this part of Strawberry Bay worked long hours at demanding, often labor-intensive jobs. The kind of jobs that left little money, time or energy for the kind of niceties found on the pages of *Martha Stewart's Living* or *Better Homes & Gardens*.

Elena climbed the chipped cement steps to Logan's house and knocked briskly on the front door. When there was no answer, she let out a relieved breath and searched her pockets for the house keys he had given her.

By the time she'd found them, Tyler and Gabby had joined her on the porch. Inserting the key in the lock, she hesitated before opening the door. "It doesn't look like he's home right now, but just remember we don't want him—"

"Involved," Gabby and Tyler said together.

Elena thought they were laughing at her again, so

she gave them a quelling look then pushed on the door. When the first floor appeared Logan-less too, Elena left the door standing wide open. "We might as well bring some things in before going upstairs."

They returned to the cars parked at the curb and helped each other load up. With an overstuffed duffel slung over each shoulder, a toiletries bag hanging on each elbow and two large cardboard boxes balanced in her arms, Elena led the way up the two flights of steps to the second floor. Similarly burdened, Gabby and Tyler followed her. The door to their apartment was at the top of the stairs, while Logan's was farther down the hall. Elena paused, then groaned.

"What is it?" Gabby's voice came out muffled, her face half-hidden by the boxes she carried.

"The keys are in the back pocket of my pants." Elena tried shifting the weight of her burdens to one arm. One of the duffels slid down her upper arm, nearly unbalancing her as it smacked into the smaller bag at her elbow. "I'll have to put some of this down," she muttered, trying to figure exactly how to do that in the narrow hallway.

A voice spoke in the vicinity of the top of her head. "Need help?"

Elena froze, then carefully swung toward the sound. Logan.

"I thought I heard someone at the front door but I was in my apartment on the phone."

He looked at perfect ease and perfectly decked out in a pair of heavy cotton khakis and a silky black T-shirt. His dark gold hair gleamed in the shadowy hall and Elena suddenly pictured herself as he would see her—her hair in two messy braids and her oldest jeans grubby.

"Making a hot date for martinis at the country club?" she asked, hoping she sounded more sneering than self-conscious.

He cocked an eyebrow at her, looking so cool and so amused that she wanted to kick him. "Jealous?" he asked softly.

"You wish," she retorted.

"True." His white smile deepened at the joke and she wanted to kick him again. Or kiss him. Again. He looked over her head. "Hi there, Gabby. Tyler. You two need some help? It appears Elena is her usual capable self and doesn't have a single use for me."

"We need into the apartment," Gabby answered.

"The keys are in Elena's back pocket and she can't reach them," Tyler added.

Before she could step away, threaten or even scream, Logan reached around her. Three long fingers slid inside her left rear pocket, the movement caressing her backside. "Here?" he asked innocently.

Elena stiffened. Less than ten minutes after her last vow not to involve him in her life, and he was already involved in her *pants*. Before she could betray herself and shiver, she did what she must.

She dropped everything she was carrying.

On Logan's feet.

He yelped and jumped back. She smiled sweetly and slowly retrieved her keys from her other pocket.

"You're right," she said, opening the door to her apartment with a flourish. "I don't have a single use for you."

Amusement flickered in his eyes again as he watched her shove the boxes and bags forward with her foot. "With the exception of my available—and rent-free—apartment," he said.

"You have the painting." She slid him a warning look. "For now."

Gabby and Tyler trooped inside with their burdens. Before she could follow, Logan's voice stopped her.

"What do you mean 'for now'?" he asked. "We have a deal. You get the apartment and I get the painting."

Her back to him, she took a breath, almost swooning when she caught the scent of his delicious, expensive-smelling aftershave. It reminded her of the kiss he'd given her last week. He'd smelled delicious then too. His face had been freshly shaven and she'd wanted to rub her cheek under his jaw. She'd wanted to run her tongue across his lips.

"Elena?" He said her name softly, as if he sensed her desire.

Snapping to attention, she spun to face him. She shoved her hands in her front pockets, her pose aggressive, her face scowling. She was supposed to stay uninvolved and here she was thinking things that made her knees weak. "What?" she bit out.

He couldn't ever know he made her weak.

One of his eyebrows made a long trek up his forehead, and he stepped closer to her. "Forgotten already, darling? I was reminding you of our deal. You get the apartment for as long as you and Gabby need it. I get the painting. Forever.''

She could smell him again. Her heartbeat kicked up and she had to force her gaze off his mouth. ''I've reconsidered,'' she said, tilting her chin. ''My side of the bargain is too generous. For six weeks I get the apartment and for those same six weeks, *only* six weeks, you get the painting.'' She pointedly turned her back on him and went into the apartment, pretending not to notice he was right behind her.

As his new housemates bustled about their apartment's small living room, Logan shook his head. Elena was up to her usual tricks.

She'd reneged in their original deal to irritate him. As always, she was working hard to push him away. But now he found himself with a hankering to know exactly *why* she wanted him to keep his distance. He had suspicions about that. Intriguing suspicions that had entered his mind just as he'd teasingly slid his hand over her luscious, rounded backside in ''search'' of the keys.

What he'd seen on her face in response to his touch wasn't that unsettling vulnerability in the kissing booth, it wasn't that purely physical weakness of the following day, it wasn't her customary prickliness.

Yet what had waved off her could very well be the *cause* of all that prickliness. If he was right, if what he'd briefly glimpsed was Elena responding to him as a woman…well, that was just too interesting a possibility to leave alone.

He'd spent the last few months—since the beginning of Griffin and Annie's courtship—at the mercy of Elena's beauty and her sharp tongue. Now she was living with him, and even when she moved back to her own place, her best friend's marriage to his brother would mean they'd be together often. It would be a hell of a lot easier for him if their relationship was on a more equal footing. Maybe, just maybe, he'd found the key to that equality.

So, sorry Elena. He wasn't backing off. There was no time like the present to determine whether she felt at least some of the pull of attraction that he did.

Gabby and Tyler acted as his unspoken but willing accomplices. Throwing him an assessing look, Elena's sister "innocently" remarked they could use a truck to retrieve a final few items. With a grin, Tyler one-handedly caught the pickup's keys when Logan immediately fished them from his pocket and tossed them over. They both emphatically declared the errand required only two pairs of hands.

Elena was frowning as the apartment door closed behind them. Then she turned on him like a cat about to sharpen her claws on her favorite scratching post. "What did you do that for?"

A tower of white bath towels was stacked in her arms. Ignoring the question, Logan approached her and she stepped back, until the heels of her sneakers bumped a cardboard box. "What's got you so jumpy?'' he asked, his voice mild. ''It couldn't be because we're alone, could it?''

She shook her head, her face stony. ''I don't like Gabby and Tyler alone. *That's* what I worry about.''

Logan slid his arms under Elena's and cupped her elbows in his palms. He watched her swallow.

''What are you doing?'' Her question sounded more uncertain than annoyed.

He slid his hands across her skin then lifted the towels. ''Helping out. Do you want these in the bathroom?''

She hugged herself. ''Oh. Okay. Thank you.'' He didn't think she was aware she was making little circles on her skin with her palms, right where he'd touched her. It was as if she was trying to erase the sensation—or perhaps her reaction?

He hid his satisfaction by turning in the direction of the bathroom. Once inside, he flipped on the light with his elbow, then piled the neatly folded towels on the open shelves above the commode. Turning back toward the door, he met his own eyes in the mirror.

He looked pleased. And eager.

Too pleased. Too eager.

Damn. That gave him pause...and second thoughts. A short while ago he'd broken up with his long-time girlfriend because he'd realized their relationship was nothing more than a habit. That wasn't the problem with Elena, of course, but he was supposed to be simplifying his life right now—focusing on working on the house and building his business. Nothing else.

Heading out of the bathroom, he decided then and

there against any more Elena-exploration. Because who was he kidding? Toying with her would only lead to him being ice-burned or hornet-stung or worse. This particular female regularly armed herself with foot-long, razor-sharp thorns. He'd be much better off—safer—heading back to his own apartment.

As he reentered her living room though, Elena's voice caused his feet to stumble. The sound was breathy, soft.

She was singing in Spanish.

A lullaby.

At the other end of the room, she sat cross-legged on a folded comforter, her back to him. He couldn't see what she was crooning to, but her body was curved over an object in her arms as she rocked back and forth.

Her hair was parted down the center and a braid fell over the front of each shoulder. The style left the nape of her neck bare and with his eyes he traced the fragile-looking bumps of her vertebrae. They pushed against her thin T-shirt until it disappeared in the waistband of her jeans.

A hot, heavy river coursed down his own spine. He walked toward her quietly, drawn forward almost against his will by her siren's song.

"What are you doing?" He touched her shoulder.

She jerked. A swathe of goose bumps rose on the exposed skin between her hairline and the neck of her T-shirt. Her head whipped toward him, a blush rushing across her cheeks. Her mouth opened, then closed.

"I thought you'd left," she finally said helplessly. "How embarrassing."

Puzzled, he hunkered down and peered over her shoulder. "Why? What's going on?"

She hunched over whatever was in her arms. "You're going to laugh."

"No, I'm not."

She narrowed her eyes and sent him another look over her shoulder. "If the tables were turned, *I'd* laugh at *you*."

Now he was *really* curious. "Yeah? But I'm nicer than you are."

"Nicer?" She appeared to consider that for a moment. "This from the man who eleven years ago—"

"Cut it out, Elena." It was so clear to him now that her needling was a form of self-preservation. "I promise I won't laugh."

She sighed. "I'm taking a college course."

"On top of two jobs and the volunteer work you're doing for the senior prom?"

"I'm working on my bachelor's degree one class at a time." She uncurled her body. "This semester it's Twenty-First Century Womanhood."

Logan leaned nearer to see what she'd been holding so protectively.

Against her full breasts. That was the first thing he noticed. So sue him, but this close and from this angle, they were truly eye-catching—throat-drying—the plump curves outlined faithfully in clingy T-shirt fabric. Nestled between them, Elena pressed a small blanket-wrapped bundle of twin—

"Eggs?" he asked, suddenly bewildered.

The faint beep of a wristwatch sounded and Elena stood up, her shoulder nearly clipping his nose. She walked away from him and he rose to follow her into the kitchen. He watched as she carefully placed her blanket bundle in a shoebox lined with cotton batting that sat on the counter.

He blinked. "What are they?"

"*Who* are they," she corrected. "Fred and Ethel. Fred and Wilma. Freddie and Krueger. Take your pick. I can't seem to decide."

He stared at Elena, then down at the ordinary-looking chicken eggs she was caring for as if they were…babies. "Ah. This is some kind of motherhood experiment?"

"Motherhood experience. We've been assigned to keep a journal describing what it's like to be a single parent in the era of sperm donors and multiple births." She turned her attention to her watch, resetting the alarm. "It's similar to what kids do in high schools. I'm required to spend a certain amount of time each day caring for the babies."

He thought of her singing that lullaby, her voice gentle, her pose maternal and almost…serene. It was the most relaxed he'd ever seen her. "You looked—now don't take this the wrong way—sweet."

You would have thought he'd insulted her. "I'm not sweet!"

"Well, no, not usually. At least not to me."

She tried shrinking him again with the laser beam of her blue eyes. "Not to *anyone*."

He smiled, because he liked the sound of that. Then he settled back on his heels. Even with all her thorns firmly in place, he didn't feel like leaving now. Not when he could still hear her voice in his head, not when he remembered those goose bumps that had gathered in response to his hand on her shoulder.

Just an inch, that was all he was asking. If he could prove to both of them that he could get beneath her skin just a scant inch, then he could go back to his new life a happy man, secure in the knowledge that the next time he encountered her *he* would be better insulated. The thought made his smile widen.

"What are you grinning about?" she asked.

He angled his head, considering what had prompted his change of heart. A few minutes ago in the bathroom he'd decided she was too dangerous to take any further risks with. But now that he'd caught her singing to yolks, well...

"For the first time in our acquaintance, I'm finding you kind of cute."

She blinked. "Cute?"

He wanted to laugh. Poor Elena. With her looks, men had probably been a constant source of flattery— wanted or not. But no one would ever have labeled her devastating package of femininity *cute*. She looked as if she didn't know whether to approve or be appalled.

"Really cute," he murmured.

She blinked again. "Next you're going to tell me I have a great personality."

Now he did laugh. "I wouldn't go that far."

"You're up to something, Logan."

He clucked his tongue. "So suspicious."

She shrugged. "A woman learns it young."

He realized he had her trapped between his body and the kitchen counter. Holding her gaze, he reached out a finger and drew it along the curve of her jaw.

Her eyes narrowed and she held herself still. Oh, but he would swear that stillness cost her. There was a tremor there, rigidly controlled, beneath her flawless golden skin. A quivering reaction to his presence, his touch.

His heart pumped hard against his chest, but he ignored it. This was about what *he* did to Elena. His gaze dropped to the pulse-beat in her throat. It was fluttering, fast, he thought. Very fast.

"Logan—"

"Logan!" It was his name again, but not in Elena's voice this time. "Logan!" It echoed through the first floor and then there was a heavy thumping on the stairs. "Where are you, son?"

Elena instantly twisted away from him. "Isn't that your father's voice?"

Damn. Just when things with Elena were getting interesting. Logan bent his head and took a calming breath, then another to fortify himself. "Yeah, that's him."

Logan knew why he was here, too. His father didn't take Logan's decision to leave Chase Electronics seriously because Logan had so rarely bucked his father's decisions. It wasn't that he'd been weak, Logan thought, but he *had* been lazy. He'd taken the path of least resistance for years, never realizing he was sinking further and further into boredom until he'd finally hit rock-bottom unhappiness.

He could feel Elena's puzzled gaze. "Shouldn't you tell him where you are?"

"Yeah." Logan straightened. "Hiding from him never lasts."

Chapter Four

After four days, Logan wondered if the O'Brien sisters were hiding from *him*. Living with Elena and Gabby was like living with ghosts. Their scents lingered in the hallway and the soft echoes of their voices sounded late at night and in the still-dark hours of the morning, but he never caught sight of them.

If it wasn't for the Elena-size sweatshirt he'd found on the stair landing one morning he might have believed he'd dreamed up the move-in day, perhaps prompted by the many times he gazed upon *Elena in Bed*. But any painting-inspired fantasy would surely have her moving in with *him*—or him moving in her—and the cotton sweatshirt had not only been real, but smelled really good, like that heated-flower perfume that the flesh-and-blood Elena always wore.

Still, when he unlocked the front door of his house about 10:30 on Thursday night, he blinked a few times before he accepted what his eyes were seeing— Elena slumped on the bottom step, her arms folded over her knees, her head on her arms. Overstuffed grocery bags and other paraphernalia sat at her feet.

"Elena?" He kept his voice quiet, afraid to startle her.

She mumbled something.

"Are you all right?" The door snicked shut behind him.

"Mmm." She lifted her head, her eyes half-mast and her mouth soft. "Promise you won't tell anyone I was drooling?"

It might have to be a mutual vow. Because she looked delectably appealing with her hair mussed and a sleepy half-smile on her face. Too tired to have her defenses up, let alone her claws out, Logan decided. He leaned back against the door, enjoying the moment. *Sleeping Beauty barely awake.*

"Long day?" he asked.

She lifted a hand toward her hair, then dropped it as if the move cost too much effort. "Yes. You?"

He ran his gaze over her body. She wore a long-sleeved dress of some light, silky fabric that was navy blue and scattered with dime-size white polka dots. At a stand, the dress likely ended just above her knees. But her seated position hiked up the hem to reveal a full half length of her nylon-encased thighs as well as her knees and calves. She wore sling-back navy pumps—the only thing his ex-girlfriend had shopped more for than beauty products was shoes, so he knew the correct term—that had heels three inches high and displayed a distracting amount of toe cleavage.

"Logan?"

Damn. She sounded like she was waking up a little and here he was, getting hard just looking at her feet. Pasting a concerned frown on his face, he pretended he was inspecting the hardwood floor at the bottom of the steps. "Is that a scuff mark or a scratch?" he murmured, striding forward.

As he neared, she drew in her heels and peered over her knees. "I don't see anything."

He let out a sigh. "You're right. Nothing to worry about." Hoping she took the last as a subliminal message, he dropped to the step beside her. There was nothing wrong, nothing to worry about for either one of them, in a little friendly, neighbor-to-neighbor catch-up.

"Where have you been tonight?" she asked.

He lifted the large disposable container he held. "The bachelor bag doesn't give it away?"

"'Bachelor bag'?" Her heavy black lashes slowly swept down, then up.

Sliding closer, he tapped her arm with his elbow. "Kinda like a doggie bag, sleepyhead. It's what every pitying mother sends home with her single son after a family dinner."

The corners of her lips quirked. "Ah. And how was your evening with Mr. and Mrs. Chase?"

How to explain his parents and their strange, yet

strangely contented relationship? Their distant marriage had nearly convinced his brother Griffin that the Chase men were incapable of love. Maybe Logan was partly to blame for that too. After all, he'd stuck with one woman for years out of nothing more than habit and their parents' wishes.

"My evening with Mr. and Mrs. Chase was as all evenings with Mr. and Mrs. Chase. Dad obsessively talked business and didn't listen to anything anyone else said. Mom serenely let Dad talk obsessively about business even while trying to make me feel like I wasn't one of the dining room walls."

"Serene is exactly the way I'd describe your mother," Elena said, nodding. "I bet she's rock-solid in a crisis."

"You're right. Every day is a crisis—a business crisis—for my father and she manages to breeze through it all." He frowned though, thinking that there was something different about his mother lately. Ever since his parents had celebrated their fortieth wedding anniversary a couple of months back, Logan had detected a brittleness to Laura Chase's usual equanimity.

But he didn't want to think about that, so he turned to Elena and smiled. "What about you? What's kept you out so late tonight?"

She shrugged. "The usual. Work, a parents' meeting at the high school. Grocery shopping."

"And baby-tending?"

Her cheeks flushed. "I hoped you'd forgotten that."

He didn't think he'd ever forget the sound of that lullaby and the sight of a baby blanket cuddled against her awesome breasts. But it would be a big mistake to hand over such a confession, so he lightly elbowed her again. "What? Afraid I'm going to turn you in for yolk-neglect?"

She reached down to retrieve a tote bag wedged between the groceries and set it on her lap. "Yolks happy and accounted for. See?"

The bag yawned open. He leaned over, and sure enough, the eggs' shoebox-crib was perched atop a stack of envelopes and a pile of paperwork. His gaze rose to hers, their faces just inches apart. "Yeah. I see."

He saw too that her eyelashes were so thick that the upper and lower ones tangled at the outside corners of her blue eyes. He saw that the flush hadn't yet receded from her creamy-gold skin. He saw that her tongue was pink and wet when she darted it out of her mouth to nervously lick her bottom lip.

Just like that, the big, three-story house shrank to one step, one woman, one man.

Her perfume, that scent of flowers in paradise, curled around his body, drawing him closer. He remembered he'd intended some friendly, neighbor-to-neighbor catching up and suddenly mouth-to-mouth seemed the logical method to make that happen.

Her pupils expanded. "No," she said. It was faint.

"Yes," he replied. Decisive.

She shook her head.

He was so close to her that the motion sent a lock

of her hair whispering against his cheek. His body clenched, impossibly tight, just with that mere, unintentional caress.

"I have to get going," Elena said.

He watched her lips form the words, thinking how they would feel moving against his. "After," he said. He lifted the tote bag from her lap, set it aside. Intending to turn her toward him, he circled each of her upper arms.

She jerked.

Then jerked away from him and jumped to her feet. "I said I have to go."

"Elena…"

Her mouth was set in a stubborn line and her eyes flashed blue fire. "I didn't ask for this."

"Of course, but—"

"I don't *want* this," she spat out, even more fiercely.

"Fine, but—"

"Is this—" she gestured between them wildly "—why you're letting me stay here?"

Shocked, he stared at her. "For God's sake, Elena. Tell me you don't believe that."

Instead of answering, she whirled way from him and started snatching her belongings from the floor. Groceries, tote bag, purse, they were all more than an armful and her angry movements hindered the task.

He rose and reached out to help. His hand brushed her shoulder.

"Don't!" she said, latching on to another bag of groceries.

"Let me help."

But she was in full defense mode. "I don't need any help," she said, an angry, dangerous Ice Queen. Her belongings gathered around her body like armor, she began ascending the stairs. "I'm perfectly fine by myself."

The strong words were hardly weakened when she had to make a desperate grab for her slipping purse.

It hit the floor with a solid thump and then was joined by a grocery sack. And then another.

Without waiting for her permission, he picked all three up. Without looking at her, he headed past her, up the stairs.

"I can manage. Put those down."

He kept climbing. She was still for another moment, as if flabbergasted that someone would ignore her orders, then he heard her start after him. When they reached her door, she dropped more groceries as she fumbled through her tote bag for her keys.

When he wordlessly reached down for the fallen sacks, he caught her glare. And then found himself glaring right back. "What the hell is the matter with you? Why is it so difficult to accept some simple help?"

She stilled. "I..." Her hand lifted vaguely, then she turned away to put the key in the door. With a jerky movement she unlocked it, pushed it open, then stepped inside.

He followed her, suddenly irritated and very unwilling to let the subject go. "It's the same with that insulting crack you made about me letting you stay

here because I wanted something—you—out of it."
The groceries he dropped to the kitchen countertop.
He held on to the purse, squeezing it instead of wring-
ing her lovely neck. "I offered to let you stay here
because you needed a place to live and I happened to
have an empty apartment."

His temper kindling, he stomped toward the apartment door. "For your information, I don't need to
hand out house keys in order to get myself a
woman."

"Are you saying you didn't want me a few minutes
ago when we were sitting on the step?" Her voice
was icy-hot.

It did not cool him down. He turned to face her.
"I'm sorry. All right? I'm sorry I tried to kiss you."

Her blue eyes flashed. "You heard me say no. Is
there something about that word you don't understand?"

The flames of his temper leaped. He didn't remember ever feeling this angry toward a woman. Maybe
toward anyone. He knew himself to be even-
tempered. Good-natured to a fault.

But right now there was an emotion burning
through his blood that was unfamiliar. It made the
colors in the room sharper and all his senses more
acute.

"I heard what you said," he snapped. He could
also hear her drawing air in and out, the rhythm as
fast as his own ragged breathing. "But I also knew
that your body, your blood, your desire was saying
'yes.'"

Spots of color lit high on her cheeks. "How dare you presume to know what I want?"

He rolled his eyes. "Elena, give me a break. I wasn't about to ravish you. A kiss. Just a kiss."

"A kiss," she repeated. Her breasts were heaving against her dress.

That unfamiliar, unnameable emotion surged in him and his focus tightened on the delectable, furious face of the one woman who'd been his every bad dream and every frustrating fantasy for the past months. "Yes, a kiss. A kiss that if you were honest with yourself you would agree you wanted. From me, Elena. Would that have been so bad? It's not like we're strangers."

She was frozen for a moment, then her eyes narrowed to shards of blue glass. "No, not strangers." Her hand made a quick, cutting movement. "I know you very well. You're the man who was once the high-and-mighty, heartless boy who asked me to the school prom then stood me up when you decided I wasn't good enough for you."

Logan's lungs were working like a steam engine when he shoved open the door to his apartment. He started to run his fingers through his hair but then realized he was still clutching Elena's purse.

"Damn it." He kicked the door closed behind him, then tossed the purse onto his couch and headed for the bathroom. He'd have to return her property, of course, but not until he had hold of himself.

Cold tap water filled his cupped palms and then he

dashed it over his face. When that didn't cool him down, he did it again, then stared at his reflection in the mirror over the sink.

What the hell was the matter with him? He looked the same. He looked like Logan Chase, reasonable, rational man. But too long in Elena's presence and he was like a werewolf under a full moon. *Ho-o-o-wl.*

But it wasn't his fault. She'd been sniping at him for months, getting in quick digs about standing her up at every opportunity. He might have let that go, gritted his teeth and accepted it as his due for the disaster that night became eleven years ago, but he couldn't accept the "not good enough" part.

Not that, by God. He didn't deserve that thrown at him and he couldn't let her think for another hour that it was true.

As soon as he had his temper back under control he'd speak to her again. It was time to discuss what had happened. He should have initiated the conversation weeks and weeks ago, he thought wearily. Maybe then the tension between them wouldn't have risen to this degree.

He took a breath, let it out slowly, then dried his dripping face with a towel. But it was going to be okay. Better than okay, once he cleared the air between them. He would feel like himself and once again peace would prevail in his world.

Elena took her sweet time answering his knock at her door. He remained patient though, even trying to look pleasant when she inched it open.

He had a view of the tip of her nose and half of one blue eye. "May I come in?" he asked.

"It's late."

At that, he considered just shoving her purse through the crack in the door and giving up on explanations. But already his tension was coiling again and he was so unaccustomed to feeling this wired that he knew he'd never get any sleep unless he got the words inside him out first.

"Please let me in," he said, trying to sound calm. "I have your purse and some things to get off my chest."

The door opened slowly and he stepped inside. The groceries were already put away and those papers and envelopes he'd earlier seen in her tote bag were spread across a card table in the dining area. "You have more work tonight?"

"Requests for applications for the fall semester. I never seem to get them all mailed out unless I bring some home every night." She'd changed out of her dress and was wearing low-slung plaid flannel pants that were cinched around her hips and a T-shirt short enough to reveal a half-inch of skin at her belly.

Pajamas? He shied away from the thought and watched her sit back at the card table then expertly trifold two double-sided papers and slide them into an envelope. She set it aside and picked up another set of pages.

Logan hung her purse on a hook by the door and then walked to the card table. Curling his hand on the back of one of the metal folding chairs drawn up to it, he watched her stuff another envelope. "Will you cut my head off if I sit down and help?"

She slid him a look, then one shoulder lifted in a shrug. "Earlier, with the groceries, I should have been more gracious. I'm...sorry."

Her apology should have eased his mood, but still something pumped just below the surface of his skin. Maybe because of that glimpse of her taut little belly, he decided. Or because he still had his own sorry to get through.

Ignoring the feeling, he sat down and pulled a stack of envelopes and applications in front of him. "There's not a trick to this, is there?"

She shook her head, then watched him fumble through his first attempt. When he was done, she continued looking at him, her forehead creased. "Really. You don't have to do this. I can manage without your help."

She didn't sound mad this time, just puzzled, and it was an easier emotion to confront. "I know that," he said. "But you need to know something too. There's no reason to throw my offers of aid back in my face or even make elaborate bargains in order to take what's freely given."

She blinked at him. "You mean you'll allow me to stay here without letting you keep *Elena in Bed*?"

I'm an idiot, he thought. *I walked right into that one.* "No," he replied flatly. "The painting stays where it is."

She sniffed, that one little sound letting him know what she thought of him.

His tension tightened a notch and he worked hard not to let it show. Reasonable, he reminded himself. Rational. "Elena, sometimes you make it damn hard for a guy to do you a good turn."

Her gaze was on the papers she was folding. "Maybe I'm out of practice. Not all that many have come my way."

"Guys or good turns?" The first he wouldn't believe; he didn't know about the second.

"What I'm trying to say is that I'm used to doing for myself."

"I get that. You're independent."

Shaking her head, she stuffed another envelope and moved on to the next, her movements efficient and automatic. "You don't get it. What I mean is, I have only myself to depend upon. And Gabby is depending on me too."

Logan's fingers stilled. "There's just the two of you?"

"Yes." She went about folding and stuffing as if they were talking about the weather instead of what she'd weathered in her life. "When I was sixteen my mother died and we moved from L.A. to Strawberry Bay to live with my grandmother. Then Nana passed away two years later and I was given custody of Gabby. I already had my job at the community college and I'd been paying the bills out of my salary for months."

He tried wrapping his mind around what she'd said. "You've taken care of your sister by yourself since you were eighteen and she was…what?"

"Nine." She looked up quickly, giving him a glare. "And we've done just fine, by the way."

"I know that. I've met Gabby. She's pre-med." He added that last bit because he knew it meant so much to Elena.

"Pre-med." Almost smiling, she nodded. "We did it."

Logan thought over what Elena had said. She didn't accept help well because she hadn't often been offered it. But the truth was, she'd have a blocks-long line of men queued up to fulfill her slightest fancy if she wished it. She was that beautiful.

But she scared them all off.

She hadn't scared him. Not eleven years ago, anyway.

Logan closed his eyes, guilt tasting metallic in his mouth. "Elena..." He opened his eyes. "We need to talk about that night."

Her gaze flew to his, surprise and something almost fearful on her face. "That night?" she echoed.

"Senior prom," he clarified, and saw her relax a little. He knew why. He didn't want to talk about the night they'd first met either. It had been a week before the senior prom and of all the things that were between them, that was the one he'd never examined or tried to explain.

Maybe because he knew he couldn't. Shouldn't. Whatever.

He reached out to put his hand over hers. Her fingers stilled, but she didn't look up at him. "You don't know how much I wish I could redo everything about the senior prom,'' he said.

She kept her eyes down. "Everything?"

She meant the fact that he'd invited *her* that night. "Maybe," he said, knowing he had to be honest. "Maybe if I could, I'd take that back too."

She nodded once.

He scooted his chair closer so that he could lift her chin with his free hand. "Not because I didn't want to share that night with you. But because I hate myself for the way it turned out, for hurting you."

As he'd expected, her gaze jumped to his. "You may have humiliated me, but you never hurt me."

"Come on—"

"You come on. Come on to the fact that I'd just lost my mother and been forced to start a new high school nearly at the end of the year. Come on to the fact that I was sixteen, new in town, and the hottest boy at my new campus invited *me* to his senior prom. Me."

"When I met you at that party—"

"We're not talking about that *other* night!"

"—I thought you went to the Catholic girls' school across town. I thought you were a senior too. I think you know that."

Her face flushed, though she pretended she hadn't heard him. "I bought a new dress and shoes with the babysitting money I'd brought with me from L.A. My grandmother curled my hair and Gabby painted my fingernails. They both helped me pick out a boutonniere for your lapel. Then the three of us waited for you to pick me up.''

Logan looked away, coward that he was. "I was wearing my tux. I'd washed and waxed my car, refusing to let anyone else touch it. The wrist corsage I bought you was in the refrigerator in the butler's pantry. Annie's mother was our—''

"Housekeeper, I know.''

"She saw it and said the white baby roses I'd picked out were perfect. They were tied with a gauzy blue ribbon that I thought was the exact color of your eyes.''

"You said you'd pick me up at seven o'clock,'' Elena reminded him. "And then it was seven, and then seven-thirty. At eight o'clock I thought maybe I'd mixed up the plans and I was supposed to meet you at the high school. My grandmother thought I should stay home and wait, but I couldn't believe you would have stood me up. So our neighbor drove me to school and I waited outside the dance for you. I realized right away that people were whispering about me, but I pretended not to hear.''

"You know that I eventually made it to your grandmother's.''

"You know that I eventually made it back there myself.''

"But we missed each other again when I went to school looking for you.'' Logan studied the way his hand covered hers and smiled a little. "Do you think if we'd had cell phones then that today the prom would just be a hazy, happy memory?''

"No."

He looked up and met her eyes. He even laughed. "You're right." No matter what, he would have remembered each moment with her in vivid detail.

"But we went over all this that night, when we finally managed to be in the same place at the same time," Elena pointed out. "It was about 10:15 I believe. You gave me that wrist corsage and it *was* perfect."

"You didn't give me the boutonniere. You crushed it in your hand—pricking yourself with the pin as I remember—then threw it and the corsage to the ground. You looked pretty perfect in that dress and those new shoes, by the way, even when you were using them to grind the flowers into the sidewalk." He had to grin, because he suddenly remembered how flummoxed he'd been, watching her stomp about, yelling at him in Spanish. He'd had no experience with someone so fiery and who so easily flung her emotions about.

He still didn't. "I never explained exactly what made me so late, though."

"The battle between your second thoughts and your good manners, I imagine."

"That's not true, Elena. At least not in the way you mean."

"Right."

"Fine. I'll admit I had second thoughts. I barely knew you, and it had been so...intense the night we met."

"We're *not* talking about the night we met," she said, sounding as if her teeth were clenched.

"Okay, okay." He curled his fingers around hers and wasn't surprised when her hand remained stiff in his grasp. "I was just about to leave to pick you up when my father called me into his study. An old friend had dropped by who he thought I should meet."

"You couldn't make your excuses?"

"You'd have to know my father—"

"I do know your father." Elena sighed. "Okay, I can see him corralling you, even on the night of your prom."

"His friend was just like him. The minutes ticked on and on and they kept asking me questions, bombarding me with advice. Still, I might have left if my father's friend wasn't the president of Whitford College."

Elena stilled. "Where you were going to attend the upcoming fall?"

Logan nodded. "And I was in a big battle with my father over my major at the time. He wanted Economics or Electrical Engineering and I wanted Industrial Arts. That night, my father's friend listened to me and helped me convince my father that my choice was a good one."

And then he'd run out of the house and broken several speed limits to get to Elena's, afraid even to risk an explanation over the phone. Hell only turned hotter as he missed her at the house, then at the high school. Finally, he'd sat outside her house until she'd arrived home. She'd been so angry that he'd not known what to say to her or even how to begin to make it up to her.

And she'd been so beautiful he'd found it difficult to find his tongue.

But then he'd discovered she was sixteen. *Just turned sixteen!* Her grandmother had called her inside, explaining to him in halting English that sophomores in high school had early curfews. "You should have told me your age. I was stunned."

She shrugged. "What did my age matter? You didn't think I was good enough for you."

Logan shook his head. "I swear to you, that wasn't ever in my mind. And I wish I could take back how standing you up led you to that conclusion. If I could have prevented that, I would have. But there was another obstacle between us, Elena. Much more basic than what side of town we lived on or how late I was that night."

Her eyebrows rose. "What do you mean?"

"I think we might have made it past that mess— been laughing about it now—if I'd called you again. If we'd made a date for the next night or the next week. Do you agree?"

She slid her hand from his and crossed her arms over her chest, regarding him out of narrowed, wary eyes. "Maybe. Okay, probably yes."

"Well, there's a very good reason that I didn't and it wasn't that I thought you weren't good enough for me." He paused, then confessed the truth. "It was that I thought you were too young for me...for the way you made me feel and what I wanted to do about it. For what I wanted to do with you."

Chapter Five

Elena was half a diet cola and four pretzels into her Friday-night routine when she heard a rap on her door. Startled, she knocked to the floor the paperwork she'd been looking over while at the same time watching "Jeopardy." Before she could regather the papers, the rap sounded again. Elena grumbled beneath her breath and rose to her feet.

Gabby had already left for a date with Tyler, but apparently she'd forgotten something, including her key. Elena strode across the floor and pulled open the door. "What—"

But it was Logan there, not her sister.

"—are you doing here?" she finished lamely.

"I need you…"

Her mind spun off for a delirious moment.

"...not to make a liar out of me," he finished.

She crossed her arms over her chest, immediately wary of whatever he had up his sleeve this time. Late last night she'd let him in and that had resulted in the uncomfortable rehash of their shared past.

Worse, shell-shocked by his admission that eleven years ago she'd been too young for what he'd wanted to do with her, she'd actually agreed to let that past go and be his friend!

Without waiting for an invitation, Logan strolled into her apartment and she sighed again, shutting the door behind him. In a pair of worn jeans and an oxford-cloth shirt rolled up to the elbows, he looked nothing like the scion of the richest family in town. He looked too casual for that.

But he also looked delicious. Goldenly handsome and ready to charm.

"What exactly do you want, Logan?" She didn't sound as cranky as she'd like. The fact was, whatever resentment she'd harbored, whatever image she'd created of Logan in her mind over the years since the senior prom, had mostly been put to rest months ago.

Once she'd spent a little time with him as an adult, she'd acknowledged to herself that he wasn't the snob she'd imagined, despite his family's wealth and prominence. The barbs she'd launched his way had been for self-protection. He was still too attractive and she still didn't want to risk succumbing to the feeling.

"I need you to go out with me tonight," he said.

"*What?*" Wait a minute. That was going too far.

He shrugged. "My father was on the phone, pressuring me to come by the house on some business thing or another. I needed an excuse to refuse him. I mentioned you.''

" 'No,' wouldn't work?''

"Hey, so I'm lousy at confrontation.'' His smile was unapologetic as well as beguiling. "But I'm great at the classic movies double feature at the coffee house.''

She gestured to the TV, papers, pretzels, soda. "I have my evening already planned.''

He took it in with one glance then gave her a look filled with pity. "And I'm offering you my help again—you need a more adventurous Friday night than this. Grab whatever you need. If we leave now we'll just make the first show. You can thank me later.''

"Don't think I'll fall for that.'' Elena almost smiled, but it wouldn't do for him to know how easily he could persuade her—and how she knew he was right. Her Friday night suddenly seemed pitiful to her, too. "If I say yes, I'll be doing *you* the favor, remember?''

He only smiled again. "Popcorn with real butter. Those handmade dark chocolates they sell, the ones with caramel and pecans.''

It took her two and a half minutes to get ready. It didn't require much effort, since he'd asked her for a favor and not a date. She smoothed on lipstick, but she didn't bother to change out of casual clothes. There wasn't time to arrange a babysitter for the eggs, so she put them in her tote bag and brought them along.

Even quick as she was, the opening credits of the first movie were rolling by the time they made it to Warm-It-Up, Strawberry Bay's newest ''hot spot.'' Housed in a building that had once been a movie theater, during the day the business operated as a typical coffee house from the original lobby. On weekend evenings, small tables and chairs were set up in the theater portion and the management showed a double feature of old movies.

Clutching popcorn, chocolates and drinks, Elena preceded Logan into the darkened theater. Afraid she'd end up on someone's lap if she went any farther, she dropped into a chair at the back of the room.

The movie playing was one of her favorites—the original *Sabrina*. It reminded Elena of her best friend Annie's romance with Griffin Chase. Annie's mother had been the Chase's housekeeper for years, and Annie had grown up on the estate watching Griffin and Logan from afar. In the movie, Sabrina ended up with the more serious older brother Linus, just as Annie had married Griffin.

For the first time, though, Elena focused on the younger brother in the movie, David. An unabashed playboy, David was portrayed as a charming n'er-do-well who cared only about his own pleasure.

That wasn't Logan at all. He was charming, oh yes, but she knew him to be a tireless worker. Even after less than a week in the Victorian house, she noticed remarkable changes. Despite the layers built up over the years, he was slowly but surely uncovering the house's timeless beauty and warmth.

When The End appeared on the screen, the theater filled with applause. Elena clapped too, now in such a cheery mood that she couldn't help but smile at Logan once the interior lights came up.

"I'm glad I'm here," she told him. She hadn't felt this relaxed and carefree in ages and knew it was good for her to leave her worries behind occasionally. "Thank you for inviting me."

His hand caught hers as he smiled back. It took her breath—that suave smile partnered with the hard, callused hand. "Thanks for coming."

"Well, sure." Her breath caught again as his thumb brushed over the top of her knuckles. The soft gesture from roughened skin made the sensation more than a little erotic. Looking away, she tugged her hand from his. "What are friends for?"

"That's what we are now? Friends?"

She glanced over at him. "Last night you said that was what you wanted, right?"

"Yeah, I guess I did," he said slowly. "Though I'm not yet convinced it's possible."

She automatically bristled. "You don't think a man and a woman can be friends?"

He leaned back in his chair, stretching his long legs in front of him. "If I'm the man and you're the woman—maybe not."

Elena stared at the strong muscles of his thighs encased in the soft jeans and decided to let that comment go.

There was a moment of silence and then Logan straightened. "Quick," he said. "Give me your hand again."

"Huh?" Before she had her wits about her, he'd taken possession of her fingers once more.

"Try to look like we don't want company." Logan leaned forward and put his elbow on the tabletop, then stared into her eyes. "The old man is pushy, but I don't think he'll insist on joining us on a date."

"Your father is here?" Elena glanced around.

"Don't look, for God's sake! Yes, he's here. With my mother. I told him where we'd be tonight. He's probably here to see if I was bluffing."

"Oh." Elena told herself it wasn't disappointment she was feeling. But she'd started wondering if Logan hadn't made up all that stuff about needing a date. Apparently not.

"This way, sweetheart," Logan urged. "Turn this way or he'll manage to catch your eye and come over to talk."

Elena scooched her chair a few inches to face Logan more fully. She mimicked his pose, putting her elbow on the table and leaning her chin on her free hand to meet his gaze. His eyes were almost the same golden brown as his hair. "Do you do this a lot?" she asked, wishing he wasn't looking at her with such...focus.

"Hmm?" He sent her a bemused, almost sleepy smile.

Even though she figured the smile was part of the act for his father, it made something warm blossom

low in her stomach. She frowned, desperate to tamp
the feeling down. "Do you often have women act as
a buffer between you and your father?"

"Ouch." He winced. "Still not pulling any
punches, are you?"

"I'm sorry," she said quickly, a little ashamed of
herself. She was still instinctively launching arrows
at him in order to keep her distance.

"It's all right. I do find it easier to circumvent dear
old dad instead of confronting him head-on. But it
wasn't fair to use you." He squeezed her hand in
apology. "Would you like to leave?"

Elena cursed her sharp tongue. "No. And *I'm*
sorry. I..." She didn't know what else to say. Afraid
to look into Logan's golden eyes again, she let her
gaze wander over his shoulder. "Oh! Gabby and Tyler are here tonight too."

They hadn't spotted her, Elena thought, because
they were looking *awfully* chummy, shoulder-to-
shoulder and their hands entwined. Prolonged physical contact between them was rare when they were
around her, and she'd found their casualness reassuring. They were going their separate ways come September, after all.

As she watched now, though, Gabby and Tyler
turned toward each other and kissed. It wasn't so
much sensual as sweet, but then again it wasn't the
least bit casual, either. A nervous chill rolled down
Elena's spine as the teenagers' kiss deepened.

"Oh, no," she muttered. So much for her carefree
Friday night.

"What's the matter?" Logan turned his head to follow her gaze. Then he turned back. "You've never seen them kiss?"

Elena shook her head. "Not quite like that."

"It worries you," Logan said, a statement, not a question.

"I—" She hesitated, realizing that without even thinking, she'd almost shared with him her concerns about Gabby and Tyler. It was uncommon for her to tell anyone, even Annie, about her troubles. She hated people thinking she was vulnerable to anything.

"You...?" Logan prompted.

Elena couldn't seem to keep her thoughts to herself. "I really like Tyler, I do. Have you seen his artwork?"

Logan nodded. "I saw the painting of his that hung next to Gabby's at the art show. I've also seen a piece of sculpture he did. My family knows his and my mother bought it for her sitting room last year."

"In the fall he'll go to the Acton School."

Logan let out a low whistle. "The art school? It's hard to get a spot there from what I understand."

Another chill rolled down Elena's spine. "Gabby was accepted there as well."

He was silent a moment. "But she chose pre-med at Berkeley."

Elena nodded.

"I don't understand the problem, then."

She glanced over his shoulder at the younger couple. The kiss was over, they weren't holding hands any longer, and a friend of Gabby's had joined them at the table. They looked like typical, teenage boy-friend and girlfriend again. Nothing more serious.

"You're right," she said, glad now that she'd confided in Logan. "There isn't a problem. Kids that age don't make lasting, um, connections with someone from the opposite sex."

He turned his head to look toward Gabby and Tyler's table again. "Is that right?"

"You know." She'd feel even better once Logan agreed with her. "They have their whole lives ahead of them. They can't possibly feel anything very strongly for each other."

"Is that right?" he repeated.

She frowned at him. "Gabby wouldn't allow it. They're going to be hours away from each other and she has years of schooling ahead of her."

"Pre-med." Logan watched her face closely.

"Right."

The lights flickered on and off, indicating the second feature was about to start. People streamed past them, heading back toward their tables. He released her hand. "Did you want something else before the next movie? More popcorn? Anything?"

Peace of mind would be good. Elena darted her glance toward Gabby and Tyler again. "Gabby wouldn't allow it," she said again. "She's too sensible."

As the room plunged into darkness, Logan's soft words reached her ears. "The one thing I've finally learned, Elena, is that our feelings rarely listen to our good sense."

His voice, the sentiment, they both made another shiver roll down her back. She should have never come with him tonight. Not only hadn't it freed her from her usual concerns, but Logan had managed to add to them.

Consequently, Elena didn't remember one scene of the second movie or even its title. She merely sat through it, her mind preoccupied with her worries about her sister. Of course, Logan was still able to distract her senses, especially when he slid his fingers through hers again and held her hand lightly.

She could have disengaged, but...she didn't, not until her watch told her it was time to tend the egg babies. Under cover of the darkness, she "fed" them, which basically meant holding them each for a short amount of time and recording it in her journal.

But even standing outside her apartment door at the Victorian, disengaging from Logan didn't get any easier. As she searched in her purse for her keys, instead of moving on to his own apartment, he propped one shoulder against the wall and watched.

Of course, that only made the darn keys more elusive.

She frowned at him. "Stop that," she hissed.

Oh, he tried to look innocent. "Stop what?"

She pulled out the keys with a triumphant flourish. "Never mind."

His steady regard didn't let up as she unlocked, then opened the door. "You worry me," he said.

She was in the process of swinging it shut in his

face because getting inside and getting away from him seemed like a good idea. "What?"

"You worry me."

"I don't need anyone worrying about me," Elena responded automatically, despite experiencing a marshmallow softening in her chest. She was the chief worrier, after all, and always had been. "I don't *want* anyone worrying about me."

His eyebrows rose. "Such a stubborn chin," he said, tapping the edge of her jaw with his fist. "Be careful of having a hard head too."

Elena frowned. "I don't know what you mean."

He sighed. "I wonder if that's true."

She didn't like game-playing and that's what it felt like Logan was doing. "If you have something to say, just spill it."

"All right." He straightened. "Don't you remember what it felt like to fall in love?"

Elena's stomach somersaulted. "What kind of conversation is this?"

"One I'm afraid to let you avoid."

It sounded like one conversation Elena didn't want her sister walking in on without warning as well. She gritted her teeth, recalculating the price of living in such close proximity with Logan. Judging by the determined expression on his face, it was a price that would only go up if she tried to run away from him now. Grimacing, she held the door open. "Coffee?"

He stepped inside. "I don't want anything."

She slid him a look. "Except to keep me up nights."

That brought a smile to his eyes. Golden eyes. Warm. Elena experienced that traitorous softening again and she found a wall to brace herself against.

"I asked if you remember falling in love, Elena."

Her gaze shifted away from his. "That's a very personal question, Logan."

"You think? Even when I was there?"

At that, she had to look back at him, but then she couldn't look away. "Quite an assumption." Instead of sounding cool and detached, the words came out stiff and false.

"That night—"

"You promised we wouldn't talk about that night!"

"—we fell in love." He shoved his hands in his pockets. "You and me, Elena. Can you deny it?"

Neither of them had ever affirmed it before—at least not aloud, not to each other. Her mouth dried and she was glad of the supporting wall behind her. "That was a long time ago, Logan. We were young."

He nodded shortly. "As I said before, you were too young."

But despite how long ago it was and despite how much more cynical she was now, her memories of her feelings that night were crystal-clear. New to Strawberry Bay, she'd gone to a party with a girl from the apartment building next door and the girl's group of friends, all of them seniors at the local Catholic high school.

There had been dozens of cars outside a big home in Logan's part of town. Several students from Straw-

berry Bay High had attended the party too, including
one tall and—to her starry eyes, anyway—suave Logan Chase. He'd found her standing in a corner and
charmed her with talk and then dancing and then
they'd found an isolated spot in the darkened back-
yard.

Remembering that, a blush, fierce and hot, rose on
her face.

"It was hormones." She sounded hoarse.

He laughed.

Already embarrassed by the situation and those
memories, the sound jabbed her, right where she felt
raw and tender. Her temper flared, and without thinking she flew at him—to push him out, to slap him,
who knew? He caught her by the shoulders, then slid
his hands down to imprison her wrists.

She glared up at him, her body thrumming with
anger, her breathing fast and shallow. "Let go of
me."

His face was hard and set, all good humor, any kind
of humor, had vanished. "Pretending it was something else won't make it less true, Elena. Neither will
being angry with me."

She wanted to deny her anger, but it was too late
for that. "Nobody falls in love like that," she said
instead. "Nobody falls in love that quickly."

"I knew the instant I saw you. I...recognized you,
even though we'd never met."

She wrenched from his grasp and half turned away
from him. "I don't know why you bring it up now.
That was years ago."

"You know exactly why I'm bringing it up. Because I don't think you should belittle or underestimate what Gabby and Tyler might feel for each other."

"You don't know them."

"You're right." His voice was soft. "But how about you? Are you so sure you know what's in their hearts?"

"Of course." Her hand flew out in a dismissive gesture. "Anyway, young love doesn't last, right? And passion dies too."

"Love, maybe. Passion?" His hand clamped down on her shoulder. "Why don't we test your theory?"

She was spun toward him even before his meaning sank in. Her spine stiffened and she opened her mouth to fling a cutting comment his way. But the look in his eyes stopped her, taking her breath. Their golden color molten now, his eyes mesmerized her as they drew nearer and nearer. She closed her own to avoid the spell.

And was bewitched by his lips instead.

It was a sweet kiss for a moment, gentle, but then she felt as if his mouth lit her on fire. A flaming shudder rolled down her spine and he jerked her close. She shuddered again, and his hands tightened their grip on her shoulders.

His tongue slid inside her lips. Elena welcomed it with a moan. Suddenly she had to get closer to him, she had to know if his heat matched her own, so she pressed herself against his chest and twined her arms around his neck.

He groaned deep in his throat, and she felt the sound with her body as much as she heard it. It told her he was affected too, that he was already edging, as she was, toward the brink of control. Almost wild. *Wild.*

The word hit her brain like an icy blast. She threw herself back, out of his arms. Finding herself shoulders-to-wall once more, she leaned into it gratefully, panting.

Logan's chest rose and fell with his own ragged breathing. Staring at her, he shook his head. "What is it you do to me?"

She tried dredging up a scathing response. "It was your idea," was the only thing she managed to get out.

"Yeah." He shook his head again, then sucked in a long breath. "Me and my bright ideas."

Trying to banish the hot desire still rushing through her body, Elena closed her eyes. But instead of finding relief, she only found memories. It had been just like this the night they'd met, too. Out in the privacy of the darkness, he'd taken her in his arms.

She'd been kissed a couple of times before, an inexperienced—and face it—almost repulsive press of lips and unpracticed thrust of tongue from fourteen- and fifteen-year-old boys. But Logan had kissed her like a man, a man with experience, his mouth at first gently seductive.

Then as now, it had been Elena who had almost immediately flared into heated desire. Elena whose passion had rocketed through her body. In one single moment she'd awakened, come shockingly alive, become a woman in the sense that she experienced a woman's needs. And also knew the man who could fulfill them.

She hung her head. "You should go."

"Yeah." He didn't move.

Her gaze stayed glued to the tips of his shoes. "Someone needs to be sensible."

"Let's take a vote as to which one of us it should be." There wasn't even a hint of laughter in his voice.

Elena swallowed. "Has it ever been like that for you again?" She should hate herself for asking.

"Elena…"

Logan's hesitation, as well as his regret and frustration, clearly communicated themselves to her. It was as if that one kiss had reopened—or reforged—a channel between them, an intimacy that would take more than a hundred kisses, more than a hundred touches, to build with anyone but him.

"No, it's not been like that," he finally answered. "Not before. Not after."

Her stomach clenched. She lifted a hand, but then let it drop. What did it matter that stirring old embers ignited new flames? Not only was she afraid to be at the mercy of such a reckless fire, there was also no time in her life for a man. Particularly no time for *this* man, who wasn't her type and—more to the point—she wasn't his.

Suddenly exhausted, she thunked the back of her head against the wall and closed her eyes. "Good night, Logan."

For a moment, silence was the only response, but then he muttered. ''Oh, to hell with it,'' she heard him say, and then she sensed his movement. He was finally leaving. Her tension released in a quick, quiet sigh.

That ended in a gasp when she found herself in his arms again. He swept her forward and crushed her against the hard wall of his chest. Then he kissed her.

No soft seduction this time. No gentle persuasion. This was the demanding kiss of a mature man who knew what response to expect. As she had feared, Elena promptly gave him that response, she couldn't help herself, her lips opening beneath the pressure of his. Her craving for Logan surged with the surge of his tongue into her mouth.

Heat flooded her body. To press her lips harder to his, she went on tiptoe and the movement caused her breasts to rub along his chest.

He made a choked sound, slanted his head to take the kiss at another angle, and then he shifted his hand to cup her breast. In a rush, her nipple tightened against his palm.

Dizzy with desire, she tilted her hips and felt him, hard and ready, against the cradle of her body. His hand left her breast and she protested, but then let the sound die as he jerked up her T-shirt.

With the fingers of one hand speared through the hair at the back of her head, he bent her back over his arm and lifted his mouth. His eyes liquid gold, he stared down at what he'd uncovered. Over the edge of her lacy black bra, the tops of her breasts lifted with each of her harsh breaths.

Need built with each fast, heavy thud of her heart. Lost in excitement, she didn't think twice about lifting one hand from Logan's shoulder to find the front clasp of her bra. His arm went steely beneath her, his pupils dilated, black consuming the gold, and his response only pushed her own excitement higher.

Impetuous, impatient, she twisted the clasp and the cups of the bra sprang apart. She brushed them away from her skin.

He seemed to drink in the sight of her bare breasts. "So beautiful."

Desire crashed over her again, raising goose bumps on her bare skin, raising her nipples to tighter points. He bent his head and took one in his mouth.

Elena closed her eyes, arching to lift herself to him. He sucked, and an intoxicating, paradoxical mix of relief and rising need shot through her.

She needed this, she needed more.

Weaving her hands through his hair, she could only hang on while he simultaneously tortured and pleasured her. It was fire, the strong suction of his mouth, the soft, sure swipe of his tongue against her nipple. It was ice, when he left that breast cooling in the air as he moved to the other.

She moaned, and he left off the gentle suction to suck more strongly. Her fingers bit into his scalp and he bit gently at her nipple.

Her pulse pounded harder. She felt it demanding and impatient at the apex of her thighs. Maybe he heard it, because his hand slid down her bare midriff to the waistband of her jeans.

Elena helped his progress. She tore at the snap, unzipped her pants herself, almost sobbed when his fingers brushed against her lower belly. His hand inched beneath the elastic of her panties, and then his fingers reached to finally find where she was hot and slick.

Lifting his mouth from her breasts, he groaned. "Elena." Her name was like a sigh before he kissed her again. His tongue slid inside her mouth. His finger slid inside her body.

They both moaned.

It was so good. Elena felt her inner muscles clasping him, felt his finger slide deep, then almost pull out, then slide even deeper. She felt as though she would die if she didn't have more. Have it all.

Desperate to get him naked, her naked, them naked together, she tore her mouth away from his. "Please, Logan."

Please, Logan. The words echoed loudly in her head. *Please, Logan.* She'd said that years ago, too. Her heart slammed against her chest.

"Please, Logan," she said again, now even more desperate. "Please, stop. *Stop.*"

He froze. Then he backed away from her until she was left standing without his touch as support or seduction. His breath was coming hard and fast and he looked dazed. Maybe that was why she wasn't embarrassed to be facing him with her shirt pushed up, her bra pushed aside, her jeans gaping.

Maybe she wasn't embarrassed because she was still wanting him so very, very badly.

But she'd had to ask him to stop. She'd *had* to. For eleven years the scales had been unbalanced, because she'd begged him then, too. *Please, Logan,* she'd said. *Please.*

But he hadn't listened.

So this time she'd forced herself to disengage from him. She'd had to turn the tables…balance those scales. She'd halted what was happening tonight because eleven years ago he'd been the one to insist *she* stop.

When she would have made love with him that night so long ago, when she'd begged him to, Logan had said no.

Chapter Six

A couple of evenings later, Elena felt satisfied enough with her attempt to balance the scales between herself and Logan that she managed—barely—not to scream when Gabby came through the door with a bag of groceries and the information that she'd invited their "landlord" to dinner.

He'd accepted.

Apparently noticing her dismay, Gabby made a face at Elena. "Come on, don't be mad. You should see how pitiful and hungry he looked."

"I'll bet," Elena replied drily. Pitiful and hungry was the way she'd expected him to look after she'd told him to stop touching and kissing her two nights before. Instead, he'd gone aloof, his expression instantly turning to a rich-boy cool that she'd been trying to emulate for years.

With a flare of teenage touchiness, Gabby spun and stomped toward the kitchen. "It's my night. If I cook, I get to invite who eats."

Elena bit back a retort. The fact that Logan had accepted the invitation meant she could only accept the inevitable and grit her teeth through the meal, anyway. To do less would be cowardly, and she refused to give him that. She'd just have to keep her distance...and keep *him* distant from her and her innermost emotions.

She knew now that the man wasn't, couldn't be, her friend, though he wasn't her enemy either. He was nothing to her, so that's all he should know of her and get from her...nothing.

No cowardice—and no kisses, either.

While Gabby made her old standby, spaghetti and meatballs, Elena set the card table for three. She refused to be ashamed of the rickety table or even of their usual paper napkins, but she folded them neatly under the forks and checked the water glasses for spots before setting them down.

A knock on the door made her jump. "I guess that's Logan," she said out loud.

Gabby was tossing a green salad and looked over, her eyebrows going up as she realized Elena wasn't planning on answering the door herself.

"He's your guest," Elena said defensively.

Gabby rolled her eyes, then abandoned the salad to head for the front door. Within seconds, Logan was inside the apartment, his smile as easy, as attractive as always.

His gaze found Elena. "*There* you are," he said.

She dropped into one of the folding chairs and slouched, stretching out her legs to cross them at the ankle. A nonchalant pose. "You need something?"

"On the grounds that it may incriminate me..." One corner of his mouth quirked into a self-deprecating smile that some women might consider charming.

Hmphf. Leave it to him to go cute when she was working so hard to freeze him out. Without another word, she jumped to her feet and hurried into the kitchen.

"Let's get this show on the road," she grumbled at Gabby. She swiped the salad bowl off the counter and marched with it to the table. Gabby followed with a deep pasta bowl filled with a pile of steaming spaghetti.

Logan sniffed appreciatively as Gabby passed, then held her chair as she sat. He headed toward Elena next, but she whipped into her own seat as if she hadn't guessed his intent.

When he laughed, as if he knew *her* intent was to avoid his nearness, she gnashed her teeth and snapped at Gabby to pass the salad. Okay, she was acting childishly, but her defenses were the only thing between Logan and losing her pride.

If he guessed the fevered dreams she'd been having every night since she'd asked him to stop, he'd probably laugh even harder.

The recent dreams were just another layer on the mortification she'd suffered for years. That night when she was sixteen she'd wanted him desperately, even though good girls weren't supposed to have those feelings. Even though good girls were supposed to be the ones to say no.

Elena stabbed at a lettuce leaf. Maybe it was genetic, she mused, that compulsion to say "yes" to the wrong man.

The phone rang. When Elena jogged to the kitchen and answered it, the identity of the person on the other end seemed like a bad omen. "Gabby," she called from the kitchen. "It's Tyler."

As she walked back to her place at the table, Elena pictured her sister's boyfriend in her mind. Blond, handsome, rich, in many ways a mirror image to the man now eating spaghetti at her table. That sense of foreboding redoubled.

She didn't meet Logan's eyes as she picked at her meal.

"Are you all right?" he asked under the cover of Gabby's phone conversation. His voice was soft. Private.

Elena scowled at him. "Of course. Why wouldn't I be?"

Instead of answering, he reached across the table with his napkin. "You missed some sauce."

She snatched the paper square away before he could touch her mouth. "I'm not a child."

His gaze on her lips, he leaned back in his chair and sent her a lazy grin. "No kidding."

She balled the napkin and barely resisted throwing it at him, even as she tried to compose her face into neutral lines. Why couldn't she handle herself more coolly around him? But she'd never been able to.

Eleven years ago, his first kiss had melted her, more, it had inflamed her. Several kisses later, she'd been so excited by his touch, so eager to know what came next in the ladder of sexual desire, that she'd been breathless when he'd slid his hand beneath her shirt and then beneath her bra.

None of her grandmother's admonitions had pricked her conscience, not when there were long, strong fingers on her flesh and Logan's praise whispering in her ears.

Her sister's reentry into the room returned Elena's focus to the present. Gabby dropped back into her seat. "Tyler's coming over for dessert," she announced.

The happy note in her little sister's voice suddenly put Elena's nerves on edge. "Didn't you see him today at school?"

Gabby paused, her fork halfway to her mouth. "Sure I did."

"Don't you think that's enough togetherness for one day?"

Before Gabby could answer, Elena's watch alarm pinged. With a sigh, she pushed back her chair and got up to fetch her shoebox with the egg babies. Back at the dinner table, she pulled out her journal to note the date and time of the latest feeding.

"How are the twins doing?" Logan leaned across the table to peer into the shoebox. "Hey—" he fished out one of the eggs "—they have faces."

"Be careful," Elena warned. "That's one-third of my class grade you're holding."

He was inspecting the Kewpie-cute face painted on the surface of the egg. "Gabby, these are charming."

"How'd you know it's my work?" she asked, obviously pleased.

"Elena in Bed," he answered.

Elena looked up, a bit miffed. "What? What about me and Fred-the-Egg are remotely alike?"

Grinning, he shrugged. "I don't know. Maybe if I slept with Fred, I'd have a good answer."

"You've never slept with me!" she exclaimed, snatching the egg out of his hand.

Gabby and Logan exchanged glances, then laughed. At Elena's expense. When she scowled at them, they laughed even harder.

"Have you forgotten where my painting of you is hung?" he finally got out.

In his bedroom. Directly opposite his bed. Feeling awkward and embarrassed, she bent her head and pretended intense concentration on the tending of her babies.

Logan continued consuming his massive portion of food. "When did you start painting?" he asked Gabby, spooning another helping of spaghetti onto his plate.

She shrugged. "I remember loving those watercolor sets little kids get. You know, the ones made out of aluminum with squares of dry paint and tiny brushes."

Elena glanced up. "Before you were even old

enough for kindergarten, you painted a landscape on the closet door of our room," she said. "Mama was so mad, because she was afraid we'd lose the security deposit."

"I can top that," Logan said, shaking his head. "My grandfather gave me a beginning woodcarver's set. I carved my name in several pieces of heirloom furniture before my mom found out and took the tools away. I wasn't allowed to play outside with Griffin for two weeks and I had to go into work with my father on Saturdays and Sundays for a month."

"Ouch," Gabby said. "Did you get your wood-carver's set back?"

"I have no idea what happened to it," Logan replied, a faraway look on his face. "I don't think I ever asked." Then he blinked and smiled at Gabby. "I don't know much about art, but I can say that from one person who works with his hands to another, you have a remarkable talent."

Her face turned pink. "Thanks," she said. "I love to paint."

"You *love* the idea of being a doctor," Elena automatically reminded her. "Don't ever forget that."

Two pairs of eyes turned on her, one blue, one brown. "They're not mutually exclusive," Gabby said, her voice tightening. "Can't you lighten up for even a minute, Elena?"

"Not when it comes to your future," she replied. "Not when it's so important."

Gabby let out a long breath. "Okay. Fine." She

stood up. "I think I'll go over to Tyler's instead of having him come over here."

Elena frowned. "Gabby…"

Her sister stiffened. "Don't start with *that* again, Elena."

"What?"

"Don't start about me and Tyler." Gabby's face flushed and she sounded annoyed. "You're not my parent."

"No, but I'm the closest thing you have to one," Elena retorted, trying to hold on to her own temper. "I'm just trying to make sure—"

"That I don't jeopardize my future as Gabriella O'Brien, M.D." Gabby's eyes were blue fire, but her voice now cooled to ice. "You want to be sure I don't get off the course you've set by getting caught up in my painting or getting caught up by a man who will dump me the way our father dumped our mother."

Before Elena could think of an appropriate response, Gabby was already at the front door. "Well, I'm tired of that boring old story. Maybe you can interest Logan, but I'm done with it."

Logan. As the realization that he'd witnessed the embarrassing exchange sank in, the front door slammed shut behind Gabby.

"Well." Not knowing what else to do, Elena stood and began stacking plates, looking forward to escaping alone to the kitchen.

But Logan instantly followed her lead.

She shook her head at him. "You don't have to help."

"I want to."

She shook her head again. "Really. It's my dish night. But I…I should apologize for what we just put you through."

"Would you like to talk about it?" he asked quietly. "My shoulder is perfectly willing to be cried upon."

"Cry?" Not in front of him. Not ever. Her spine steeled. "I'm not much of a crier. Especially over a minor skirmish with my little sister."

His golden eyes searched her face, but then he shrugged. "You know, Elena, you are the toughest cookie I ever met."

She smiled at him. "Now you're talking." When she carried the dishes toward the kitchen, she didn't even mind him trailing behind her. A tough cookie like herself could handle him and think about the argument with Gabby later.

While Elena started filling the kitchen sink, Logan leaned against the opposite countertop, as if he didn't have another place in the world he'd rather be. "I assumed your father had passed away," he said after a few minutes.

Elena stiffened, then forced herself to relax. She'd just said she could handle Logan, right? "No. He's a lawyer in his family's firm in L.A."

"*His* family? Isn't that family yours too?"

She was glad her back was turned, because tough cookies didn't show emotion and she didn't know if she could talk about her father without doing so. "My father and his family want to forget all about me and

Gabby. He took a job with legal aid and married our mother—she was a cocktail waitress at his favorite Mexican restaurant—as rebellion against his stuffy parents. For the next ten years or so, my mother and father lived together in wedded un-bliss."

"Then what happened?"

She shrugged. "His snobbishness overcame his need to rebel? He was more embarrassed of us than he was interested in making a point? You'd have to ask him. I only know that when Gabby was born, he gave up slumming, his Mexican-American wife and his two daughters. I believe he's now a civil litigator and the proud father of three sons in prep school."

"Jesus, Elena." Without her noticing, Logan had snuck up behind her, and now he touched her hair. "I'm sorry—"

"Not for me." She whirled to face him, defiant. "You better not be sorry for me."

He tucked her hair behind her ear. "No, sweetheart. I'm sorry for your father. Sorry that he doesn't know Gabby. Sorry that he doesn't know you."

Elena swallowed, fighting off the weak, silly urge to step into Logan's arms. *He* wasn't supposed to know her either! She was supposed to be keeping him at a distance and not letting him past her guard.

She firmed her jaw and looked into his eyes, willing herself to give nothing away. "I think that you should go."

Logan gazed at the cool mask of beauty that was Elena's face. She was kicking him out again.

Damn her.

He'd gone quietly, even willingly, the other night, though she'd been half-naked in his arms. With the taste of her perfumed skin still on his tongue, he'd managed to walk away from her.

Conversation with Elena, let alone near-copulation with Elena, was a complication to his life he'd known he didn't need at the moment.

He'd been aware too, that he'd left her as sexually frustrated, as sexually hurting as he was himself. A consolation. Even retaliation—it only seemed fair that they both suffered.

But what she was feeling now wasn't physical pain. He could tell she was emotionally hurting from her argument with Gabby and from talking about her father. It pissed him off that she wouldn't even admit it—or give him a chance to comfort her.

"You won't let anyone get too close, will you Elena?" he said tightly.

Her expression didn't flicker. "I'll walk you to the door."

How many feet away could it be? Twenty? Yet with each step he felt another surge of that unfamiliar and hot, although also strangely exhilarating, emotion rise within him.

When she put her hand on the doorknob, he thought of the beautiful girl in the ice-blue prom dress who had snatched the corsage from his hand. Emotions rippling across her face, she'd thrown it down to grind it into the cement with her shoe.

He'd been intrigued and awed by all that honesty

and temper, so different from the iron fist that his family used to control their feelings.

But now, he thought, despite the habitual verbal barbs and the occasional flash of real temper, she had grown to be like them. Under that impenetrable outer shell, she held everything she felt close to her heart. She wasn't like the fiery Elena he remembered at all.

And because he thought he might be in some way responsible for that change, he only felt angrier. She drew open the door. He slammed it shut with the flat of his hand.

"No," he said.

She turned those cool blue eyes on him. "What?"

"I'm not going to let you push me away like this again."

Oh, she was good. Her eyebrows rose in a way perfected to frighten off the male half of the world. It was a look that could shrivel a man—his ego as well as his erection—unless that man knew what was underneath all her aloof condescension.

Wariness. Hurt. Her own fear, he suspected.

He leaned against the door, his adrenaline pumping, something telling him that a corner could be turned here if he pushed her. Pursued her.

Reaching out, he cupped her cheek with his palm. Her skin was velvety and warm. He remembered cupping her breast, the skin there was velvety too, and he'd felt her heartbeat racing against his fingertips.

She didn't budge, but there was just the slightest catch in her voice. "You don't want to do this, Logan."

Rationally—no. The good-natured, even-tempered Logan he'd been all his life was somewhere inside him, pointing out in reasonable tones that involving himself with Elena would only mess him up. But that voice was part of the same analytical, common-sensical Logan who had stayed chained to a desk job at Chase Electronics for too many years.

Maybe it was time for a different kind of thinking. Or, better yet, not thinking at all.

His thumb stroked across her cheekbone. "This isn't just for me," he said.

Uncertainty flickered in her eyes and he delighted in it. She licked her bottom lip. "Oh, I suppose I should be honored that you want…that you want to spend time with me?"

She was still trying so hard to push him away.

Ha. "Give an inch, Elena," he whispered, his thumb brushing across her face again. "You don't have to give it all, just an inch."

"I don't know what you want." Now she sounded nervous, almost defensive.

He pressed, knowing this was the opening he needed. "I want you to talk to me, Elena. Admit what's going on with you and Gabby. Admit what's going on with you and me."

She stiffened against his hand. "You know there's no you and me."

"You know there could be." He took a step toward her, his gaze never leaving hers. "I thought the attraction was just an echo of the past. But I was wrong, because it's not going away and it's only getting harder to ignore.''

"Well, I'll do fine without scratching that particular itch, thank you very much."

"Damn you, Elena." His temper burned and he heard that wolf begin howling inside his head. Only *she* brought out in him something so untamed. "I'm not going to let you drag it down to that level."

She jerked her face away from his hand. "What other level is there?"

Anger flared again, but this time not at Elena, but at whatever—or whoever—had made her so distrustful. He grabbed her chin and turned her face his way again. "Take something from me," he commanded her.

She blinked. "What are you talking about?"

"Not just about kisses, caresses, sex. I'm *offering,* Elena. Giving. Take my comfort, take my support, take me as someone to share your worries with."

Her eyes widened. Emotions rippled across them, like disturbances in the depths of an icy lake.

"Let me in, Elena. I want to know you again. *Know* you."

Elena shook her head. "We can't be friends. You know how ridiculous that is."

If not friendship—because she was right about that—what *did* he want from her? Peace, he thought, and simplicity. Not that he'd ever have either with Elena buzzing about, bringing up old memories and past regrets. Not with her beautiful face and stubborn heart as a constant source of howling frustration.

"It's just as ridiculous to think we're going to keep avoiding whatever we already are," he said slowly. "And what we never became. I think we should play out what's between us this time. Finish it, once and for all."

"Finish it once and for all," she murmured, as if trying out the idea.

He saw the surrender on her face and his heart kicked into high gear. This made so much sense.

Then she bit her bottom lip. "Let me…let me think about it."

God, could she never do anything the easy way? The wolf howled again and he clung to control by his fingernails. "Fine." He was on his way out of her apartment before he did something stupid like punch a hole in a wall…or beg. "Let me know when you've decided."

Chapter Seven

By late afternoon the following day, though Logan's body was exhausted he continued working, hoping to tire out his brain as well. He'd made progress on stripping the paint from the wainscoting in the dining room. Now he was positioned at the far end of the first-floor hall, replacing water-damaged floorboards.

He measured the length he needed to cut, then measured again as a double check, scribbling the number on a scrap of wood. Normally he could keep something so simple in his head until he reached the well-lit location where he'd set up his chop saw, but he was too preoccupied today, thinking of Elena.

She'd gone ghost on him again. Even though he'd risen with the sun, she'd already left the Victorian by the time he'd made his bleary-eyed way out of his own apartment. Though he'd caught Gabby before she'd left for school, she hadn't been much help in Elena mood-analysis.

There had been a mischievous spark in her eyes, however, when she'd shared her sister's schedule for the day. Elena would be back around 6:00 p.m.

Logan planned on being showered and irresistible by then. He'd greet her with a smile and insist on taking her out to dinner. They had important matters to discuss.

The latest whine of blade cutting oak was just diminishing when he heard a knock on the front door. He'd left it propped open to dissipate some of the fumes from the paint-stripper he'd been using, so he just yelled, "Come in," and then headed in the direction of the foyer.

Jonathon Chase stepped over the threshold, looking as freshly pressed and as tightly necktied as…as Logan had looked for too many years. Conscious of the coating of sawdust on his forearms and hands, he grinned to himself as he reached for his father's outstretched palm and shook it.

Handshake over, Jonathon looked down at his gritty fingers, perplexed.

"Sorry, Dad." Logan bit back another smile and reached for his handkerchief. It came out of the back pocket of his jeans in a flurry of more sawdust. "Oops."

"Never mind." His father had already found his own and was wiping his hand clean. "How are you, son?"

"Busy." Avoiding looking at the sheaf of papers under his father's arm—Jonathon was continually trying to draw him back into the family business with new proposals or projections—Logan shoved his handkerchief away. "Would you like to see my progress?"

The question seemed to throw the older man off his stride. "Well, uh, sure."

Logan took him on a brief tour of the downstairs rooms. "I'm hopscotching around, trying to determine exactly what needs to be done and how long it will take to do it."

"It looks like a hell of a mess to me," his father said, staring at the half-peeled wallpaper in the parlor.

Logan shrugged. "Yeah. More mess to come if I'm going to turn this floor and the third into more apartments. But now I'm thinking of scrapping that idea."

Jonathon pressed his lips together and nodded with satisfaction. "You want your desk back at Chase Electronics."

Logan half-smiled. "No, Dad. I'm thinking of turning this house into my company headquarters. Business offices on the first floor, living quarters on the second and third stories."

"You need business space?"

Logan nodded, holding on to his pleasant expression. "I've got an architect coming on board with me in three months as well as a couple of subcontractors who are interested in full-time employment instead of scrambling for job after job."

"Someone has to find the work," his father pointed out.

"That will be me." Logan waited for Jonathon to launch some doubts on that score, promising himself he wouldn't bother to tell his father he already had two large renovations lined up and the verbal promise of a third. He wouldn't bother telling the old man that he still planned on doing a lot of the work himself, too.

Instead, his father surprised the hell out of him by merely nodding. He looked away, then back at Logan. "Have you spoken with your mother lately?" he asked abruptly.

Logan blinked. "Not since we all had dinner together the other night."

Jonathon nodded again but then let silence fall.

Puzzled, Logan cleared his throat. "Uh, Dad. Did you drop by for some reason? I notice you have papers with you." It's not as if he'd avoid whatever his father's purpose was anyway.

Jonathon blinked, seeming to awaken. Then he looked down as if noticing the papers for the first time. "I don't know why I brought these in with me," he said slowly. "I was on my way to drop them... somewhere."

It sounded as if Logan's mind-like-a-shark father couldn't remember where that "somewhere" was. Alarms pinged. "Are you feeling okay, Dad?"

His father shook his head, as if clearing it. "Of course. I'm okay. Everything's okay. Everything will be perfectly okay as soon as you give up this foolish notion and come back into the fold.''

Over his dead body, Logan thought, but he smiled pleasantly yet again. ''No, Dad. I'm going to hold on to this foolish notion, but thanks for your good wishes all the same.''

His father didn't even catch the edge of sarcasm in Logan's voice. After a few more minutes he left, with only another odd comment about Logan's mother. ''She wasn't home on Monday night for martinis.''

''God,'' Logan muttered, as he returned to his work. ''No martinis on Monday night.'' How did the old man's world keep turning?

It was *his* world that recaptured his thoughts, though. More precisely, how it would be changed depending upon what words would drop from the delectable lips of one blue-eyed brunette when she returned home today. He supposed she might assume she had more time to make her decision, but Logan was discovering he wasn't as patient a man as he'd always thought.

''Logan?'' The sound of that familiar voice calling through his still-open front door was almost eerie. It was the voice of the personification of that very patience.

''Cynthia?'' he called out. ''Is that you?''

He made his way back to the foyer, and sure enough, it was Cynthia Halstead. Though rumors of their long-expected engagement had always been greatly exaggerated, he *had* dated her almost exclusively for several years.

Standing in the entry, she tossed back the long fall of her straight blond hair and gave him a tentative smile. "So this is where you work?"

"And live," he reminded her. They'd ended their romantic liaison before his change in careers and residences, but he still occasionally talked to her on the phone.

Their relationship had been so cool it hadn't adversely suffered from the breakup, strange as that might sound. The people most disturbed by it seemed to be their parents, who had dreamed up a marriage when Logan and Cynthia were in their cradles.

"How are Peter and Meredith?" he asked politely. "And your brother?"

"P.J.'s fine. Mother and Dad..." Her slender hand flapped, and then she stepped past him. Her walk was fluid, one of those runway-model saunters that ate up space but didn't seem to go anywhere at the same time.

Logan trailed her passively. Cynthia *was* a part-time model and he was accustomed to the way she used movement to rev up her thought process. She wasn't dumb—and hated that stereotype—but if she wasn't moving, she had a tendency to shut down her brain. She'd shared with him once her technique for sitting still in a makeup chair or under a photographer's lights for hour upon hour. To keep herself from screaming in boredom, she'd flat-line her mind, achieving an almost catatonic state, sort of like a bear going into hibernation.

Of course, no one with those miles of long hair and

legs resembled a bear, but the simile had stayed with him all the same.

Once she'd made a complete tour of the downstairs, she whirled to face him. "I was really, really angry with you."

He stared at her. "Huh?"

"When you broke up with me."

"Hell, Cynthia." Flummoxed, he pushed both hands through his hair, not even thinking about the sawdust covering them. He'd thought she'd taken their breakup so well. "Why didn't you say anything?"

She shrugged. "You talked about it as if it was a mutual decision we were making. I had too much pride to tell you that my mother had already booked a room for our wedding reception and that we had started shopping for wedding gowns."

Logan's jaw dropped. "What?"

Her shoulders moved up and down again. "Places to hold wedding receptions for a thousand guests are hard to come by around Strawberry Bay. You have to book over twelve months in advance."

A *thousand* guests? He shook his head. "I—I don't know exactly what to say." Marriage? To Cynthia? The idea terrified him.

She smiled. "Say that you'll hold the first Saturday in February next year free."

He stopped himself from immediately declaring that in February of next year he'd be deep in training with the French Foreign Legion. "Tell me...tell me you don't mean..."

Her smile widened. "I'm getting married."

He backed up so quickly he tripped over his own feet. "You're..."

Cynthia laughed. "You should see your face!"

Logan pushed his hands through his hair again. "I'm not following you."

"I'm engaged to marry Nicky LeGrand."

Logan stared. "Nicky 'Let Me Care for Your Lawns' LeGrand?"

She lifted her chin. "You have a problem with that?"

"No! No, of course not." Except that the notion of Cynthia marrying someone else made him almost faint with relief. "I didn't know that you and Nicky were even acquainted, much less dating."

Her pale complexion flushed bright red. "He's been taking care of the grounds at my parents' while our regular man recuperates from back surgery."

Logan bit back a grin. The only daughter of Peter and Meredith Halstead was engaged to marry the gardener! "I wish you the very best, of course, but...but..."

"How are my parents handling it?"

He nodded.

Cynthia's smile turned mischievous. "To quote my father: 'At least he's not the pool man.' My mother appears immensely relieved I'm not pregnant and don't plan to be before the wedding. My cousin DeeDee just took her new baby and eloped with the driver of the diaper service truck, so I look positively saintly in comparison."

Logan laughed. "The beauty of a small town— someone's private business is always more jaw-dropping than our own."

"That's one of the reasons I'm here," Cynthia said.

"You came to tell me about your cousin DeeDee?"

She shook her head. "No. I came because I heard that Elena O'Brien is living with you."

"She's not *living* with me," he corrected hastily. If that got around, Elena would skewer him. "She and her sister are staying in a separate apartment from mine."

"Oh." Cynthia looked disappointed. "I thought we could exchange congratulations. And I wanted to thank you, too."

"Thank me for what?"

"For showing me what passion is." She grinned.

"*I* showed you?"

"In a backhanded sort of way. I thought the comfortable relationship we had was something to build a lifetime on. But then I found Nicky...." Her face glowed. "It's not comfortable, it's not even easy, but he makes me feel so *alive*."

Logan shook his head. Cynthia had always been as cool as the cucumber masks she slathered on her face every Sunday night. It should be impossible to consider her a passionate woman—if he hadn't seen the look in her eyes when she mentioned her fiancé's name.

"I'm so happy for you," he said, though her definition of a "not comfortable" and "not easy" passion made him distinctly *un*comfortable. ''Come here and give me a hug.''

If Logan had wanted to make Elena's life miserable, he couldn't have done anything more than offer himself up—and then leave it to her to decide whether to take him.

She hadn't slept a wink the previous night and she'd been distracted all day long.

At noon, she'd run from her day job to the high school for a meeting with the senior prom committee. What a waste of time that had been. She couldn't recall a thing they'd decided and she was going to have to remember to abase herself to the ferocious secretary of the committee to get a copy of the meeting minutes ASAP.

For all she knew, she'd volunteered to chaperon, and she'd promised Gabby she'd do anything but that.

Now, here it was, a beautiful May evening, and she was no nearer to a decision regarding Logan. She hesitated at the bottom of the steps leading to the Victorian's wide front porch. Something told her he'd want to know her decision the instant she walked inside.

If only she wasn't such a lousy judge of men! Following the disaster with Logan, she'd steered clear of boys until her senior year in high school. Then she'd spent a few months dating one of those bad-boy types—no coincidence that he was the exact opposite of Logan—but he'd abruptly stopped calling when her grandmother had died and she'd taken on the responsibility of her sister.

Four years later, a burgeoning relationship had fallen to ruins when the man realized Elena didn't have time to play corporate girlfriend, let alone corporate wife.

After that, men hadn't seemed worth the trouble. She'd been a busy woman with a little sister to raise. The men she met never paid any attention to Gabby and they'd hardly seemed interested in Elena herself. They'd only seemed focused on the way she looked.

But Logan…Logan seduced her with his caring.

It frightened her, because his support and strength sounded so appealing. What if she came to depend upon it and then he left her?

And leaving her was exactly what *was* going to happen. He'd suggested they get close so that they could *finish* things between them, after all.

Would that really work? Could she spend time with him as a way to achieve a clean ending? It sounded risky, but there was the fact that Elena's best friend was married to his brother. If she and Logan didn't do something about the ever-present tension between them, there would be stressful social situations for years to come.

A warm breeze blew across her face. It smelled like gardenias and it instantly brought to mind Annie's wedding. They'd both carried bouquets of the fragrant, creamy-white flowers, and, as maid of honor, Elena had paraded toward the altar, feeling almost bride-like herself in a long satin dress. She'd dared to peek at Logan, standing as best man beside his brother, and for a second or two she'd let herself imagine it was her own wedding and she was walking forward to join her life to his.

Oh, that was such a dangerous sort of imagining! And she had to admit she didn't think these fantasies would go away unless she took drastic measures.

Suddenly resolute, Elena placed her foot on the bottom step. Okay. She'd tell him yes. She'd go along with this crazy plan because it sounded marginally better than going crazy wondering what could have been night after night.

His plan seemed the only way she could regain control of her life.

Still, her heart jumped with each step she ascended. The front door was ajar and she pushed it open, suddenly eager to see—

Logan. Logan's arms wrapped around another woman.

She froze, trying to absorb the scene in front of her. It was Cynthia Halstead, Logan's long-time girlfriend. Supposedly they'd been broken up for months, but right now Cynthia appeared to be smiling and weeping at the same time.

A happy woman.

Logan looked up, spotted Elena.

A dead man.

He murmured something to Cynthia, then dropped his arms. "You're back," he said.

Elena lifted her eyebrow. Slowly. It was really, really important to play this well, she told herself, even though this was the same rat who supposedly wanted *her* to fall into his arms. "Is that a problem?"

His eyes narrowed. "No. No problem at all. Cynthia and I were just saying goodbye."

Elena shifted her gaze to the other woman and smiled at her. A genuine, pleased-to-see-you smile.

She hoped.

"Hi, Cynthia. You're not leaving on my account, I hope."

There were still happy tearstains on the blonde's cheeks. She glanced at Logan, back to Elena. "Oh, no. I've got to get home. Immediately."

Short of video footage showing people fleeing from tornadoes, Elena had never seen anyone move so fast. One moment Cynthia was there, the next she was just a memory of unfairly long legs and Shalimar perfume.

Wearing a bemused expression, Logan looked off in the direction she'd taken. "Cynthia was never one for confrontation," he murmured. "We have that in common."

Elena thought of glaciers. The frozen tip of Mount Everest. An ice pick through Logan's heart. Oops. She shouldn't care that much about him, right?

"Confrontation?" she scoffed. "What on earth are you talking about?"

"Confronting you. You're angry."

"Not at you." At herself. For being so stupid, so *stupid,* to think for one second that her luck with men, with *Logan* would change.

Logan cleared his throat. "Cynthia came over to tell me she's engaged to Nicky LeGrand."

"Uh-huh." The day that former debutante Cynthia Halstead married Nicky "Let Me Care for Your Lawns" LeGrand was the day that Elena married…married… Now was not a good time to think again of weddings and Logan.

She stalked across the foyer toward the stairs and tried to pass him.

He caught her arm. "I'm telling you, she came over to inform me of her engagement."

"Because you certainly don't read the engagement announcements in the newspaper," she said, proud of the cool control in her voice.

"Of course I don't read the engagement announcements in the newspaper." He blinked. "Engagements are actually *listed* in the newspaper?"

"How should I know?" Unless she'd been reading those particular pages every Sunday for years, searching for Logan's name. Always holding her breath, always expecting to find a box with a studio photo of him and an insipid blonde proclaiming their imminent marriage.

Elena looked down her nose at his hand on her arm. "Please release me."

"No."

She tugged. "Yes."

His jaw tightened and so did his hold on her. "No."

"Yes."

"No."

"*Yes.*" Their little skirmish might be childish, but still she was glad that she didn't yell, that she didn't scream, that she kept her voice ice-cube cold. "Let go."

"Not until you admit you're jealous."

She stiffened. *"What?"*

"You're mad that you came home and found me hugging another woman. You're jealous of Cynthia."

"Jealous of that washed-out, stuck-up, stick-figure blonde?" The cold inside Elena was melting fast and she couldn't seem to stop it. "Don't flatter yourself."

He grinned. "I do find it flattering."

Years of hard-won control and hard-edged iciness were on the verge of evaporation. She muttered something.

"What?" he asked, humor still glinting in his eyes. "What was that?"

She clung to the remaining slivers of her dignity. "A very bad Spanish curse word."

He grinned again. "It occurs to me that you wouldn't be so mad if you hadn't come home intending to agree to my plan."

She twisted out of his now-relaxed grasp, then took a tiny step back and widened her eyes in disbelief. "Are you still talking about your begin-it-to-end-it plan? Come on, doesn't that sound just a little bit nuts to you after a good night's sleep?" She hoped he assumed she'd slept the slumber of a peaceful baby.

"Maybe, if 'beginning' was at issue," he replied. In the blink of an eye, he reached out to circle her waist with his palms. "But we're already hip-deep, don't you think?"

If she could think at all, she might think she was

in big, big trouble. But Logan's hands slid down to those hips he'd mentioned and when she put her own hands up to fend him off, they didn't do more than rest against his chest. She breathed him in and it was the scent of his expensive aftershave and sawdust and maybe just the slightest hint of...Shalimar.

Remembering she should be mad, she scowled up at him. "Tell me the truth. Are you still seeing Cynthia?"

He shook his head. "No. Cross my heart and hope to work for my father again. Like I said, she stopped by to tell me about Nicky."

Elena bit her bottom lip, trying to keep her mind on the subject and off his hands. His fingers were splayed across the curves of her bottom, while his thumbs were making lovely, attention-demanding circles just to the inside of her pelvic bones.

She was wearing a long skirt of thin cotton and now she wished she'd worn something thicker, heavier—armor perhaps—that would better protect her from his touch. "You need to stop that," she said hoarsely.

His nostrils flared. "Stop what?"

"I can't think."

"That's the idea, honey. I've decided we've both been thinking too much all these years."

But those years had taught her lessons, too. She was much, much warier now. "Even if I do agree to this plan of yours, we first have to negotiate the terms."

He laughed. "You're making it sound like a surrender."

"It isn't?" She lifted an eyebrow. "Or is that point number one, no surrender?"

His eyes narrowed and his laughter abruptly died. "I'm not following you."

"Yesterday you said you wanted to 'know' me. What does that mean, exactly?"

He shrugged. "That you stop avoid—hell, that you stop running from me. That you talk to me."

"That's it? No sex?"

Laughter once again warmed his golden eyes. "I'd agree to that, Elena, but we'd both probably make a liar out of me. However, I'm not obligating you to a single thing you don't feel like sharing with me—and that includes your body. But I do want some of your time. I'll be content with where things go from there."

"Things" would go straight to sex. She grimaced. "Why is it you sound like the spider?"

"I don't know." His fingers flexed against her backside to draw her closer against him. "Why are you feeling like the fly?"

Its short life span? Could she truly survive spending time with Logan again? She breathed in his woody, delicious warmth and raised her gaze from his strong throat to his mouth, and then to his eyes. "You're sure this is the way to end things between us?"

"I'm sure," he answered, but his voice was distracted as his gaze narrowed on her mouth.

Elena swallowed. "You're sure this isn't going to make things between us only more complicated?"

"I'm sure," he murmured, his mouth descending.

She frowned. Was he listening? Did he even know what he was saying? "Are you sure you're willing to be slave to my heart?" she tested, knowing that should wake him up.

"I'm sure," he said against her mouth.

He hadn't been listening obviously, but the kiss was a fine answer. All uncertainty drifted away in the sensation of his tongue slipping between her lips. She stretched upward, pulling him closer at the same time. They stood plastered together, mouth to mouth, pelvis to pelvis, and if Elena had carried a white flag, she would have been waving it with all her might.

He tore his mouth away from hers. "No." His head shaking, he pushed her a couple of inches away. "It shouldn't go like this. I thought we'd have dinner and then a movie or something..."

She wove her fingers through his thick, dark-gold hair. Oh, it was so good to be able to touch him at will. She could do that now, she didn't have to hold herself back, and it was the sweetest of liberties. Her smile felt as if it could light the world. "Okay."

He cocked his head. "The dinner or the movie or the something?"

She smiled wider. "Okay."

He groaned and grabbed her close again. "You know, it's too good. Imagine it. This big house and just you and me."

She rubbed her cheek against his chest. "And Gabby."

"And Gabby," he repeated.

"Yoo-hoo!" A voice warbled through the front door that wasn't completely closed. "Lo-gan! Logan!"

Elena and Logan sprang apart. She glanced at him. "And, um, who else?"

He frowned. "Would you believe...my mother?"

Chapter Eight

Logan considered barring women from his house. But it was too damn late, because they'd already wreaked havoc on his whole day. First Cynthia, then Elena—who admittedly wreaked havoc on him no matter where she was—and now...now his mother.

He set her matching pieces of luggage at the bottom of the staircase leading to the upper floors and studied her habitually serene face. "Mom, not that I don't love you and everything, but why are you moving in with *me?*"

She smoothed her silver-blond hair away from her face, then straightened the sleeve of her silk blouse so it rode the edge of her platinum-and-diamond watch. "I explained that to you. I can't live with your father right now."

As much as he sympathized with the sentiment, his mother still wasn't making sense. "Sure, Mom, but there are hotels. Your house in Hawaii. That new resort just outside of town."

His mother's chin firmed. Strange, he'd never seen her look so stubborn. "Are you saying I'm not welcome here?"

"Jeez, Mom, of course not." He mentally rolled his eyes and tried not to look at Elena, who was standing above him on the landing. God forbid he tangle with another prickly female today. "It's just that my apartment isn't very big and Elena and Gabby are in the free one for the time being."

His mother lifted her manicured hand in a movement that was at once languid and commanding. "Take them up, Logan, dear."

Cursing inwardly, he regathered her suitcases and started up the stairs. He passed Elena on the landing and bared his teeth at her in what he hoped his mother would mistake for a smile. "This is your fault," he muttered.

"How could you say no?" she whispered back. "She's your *mother*."

He didn't care if she was the mother of all mankind. If it had been left up to him, he would have seen her settled in the penthouse suite at the Bay Inn. But while his mother had been explaining she'd left the estate and wanted to move into the Victorian, Elena had been looking at him with those wide blue eyes of hers. He'd thought of all that she'd done for her little sister, and he'd been loathe to shrug off his mother and her problems.

Except, damn it, now they were *his* problems too, and they were going to impact his plans for Elena.

He kicked open the door to his apartment, then stalked into the extra bedroom to drop the luggage once again. When he returned to the living room, it was to see his mother looking around with appreciation, Elena hovering behind her.

"Logan," his mother said, "I had no idea what a beautiful house this is. You've done wonders."

He grunted. "Reuben, the guy who owned it before me, remodeled this apartment and the other one."

"But Logan has done all the work on the first floor," Elena put in. "You wouldn't believe how much he's accomplished."

Sexual frustration, he could have told her, was behind all the progress. And just when he'd hoped to channel that energy into a much more natural, interesting direction...

"Mom," he said, "how long are you planning on staying here?"

"As long as it takes," she answered vaguely. She smoothed her hair and then looked down at her hands.

She was still wearing her wedding ring, Logan noted. He cleared his throat. "Well, uh, Elena and I were just about to go out and eat."

"Why don't you shower first, dear." Her gaze shifted to Elena. "Then I'll take you both out to dinner."

Several hours later he found himself sitting on the

floor in the parlor in front of the big-screen TV, surrounded by women.

It sucked.

His mother had commandeered one of the ratty recliners. Gabby and Elena squished into the other. Worse, the females had also taken over the remote control and were clicking between some made-for-TV movie starring a soap hunk they all recognized and a program that depicted a real-life labor and delivery of a real-life baby.

Just as a hospital-gowned mother-to-be emitted some spine-chilling moans, Logan heard the phone ringing upstairs.

He said he heard it, anyway.

Once inside his bedroom with two closed doors and the stairway between himself and the women, he dialed a familiar number. The housekeeper at the Chase estate answered. When he asked for his father, she said he wasn't at home. Nor was Mrs. Chase, she added in her pleasant voice.

"I know," Logan responded with a heavy sigh. Mrs. Chase had definitely moved in with him, despite all his not-so-subtle hints that she'd be more comfortable elsewhere.

Replacing the phone on the receiver, from far away he heard the sound of female laughter. Wincing, he resisted the urge to hold his aching head. What could they find so funny about he-men or human birth?

But maybe they were laughing at the great big cosmic joke on Logan. His effort to extricate himself from the family business and from family expectations had now landed him smack-dab in the center of his parents' separation—and just as he had the woman who was the ultimate, freakin' fantasy of his life inches from his bed.

Another round of laughter from downstairs made the dull pounding in his head turn to a roar.

Because Mrs. Chase was now in residence at the Victorian, Elena figured the plan of Logan's that she'd agreed to was at the very least indefinitely post-poned. She told herself she was grateful—now she could use the time to explore some very sensible and quite rational second thoughts.

But then she unlocked the front door of the house late Friday night, and found Logan in near-darkness, lying in wait for her.

She stayed where she was, hand clutching the door-knob. He was truly *lying* in wait—his long body, il-luminated by the meager glow of a light left on in the original kitchen, was stretched out on the floor at the bottom of the stairs, his head pillowed on what might be a rolled-up drop cloth. Coward that she was, she considered avoiding him by turning around and leav-ing the house. But she'd already spent ten hours at her day job followed by another two-and-a-half as-sisting the Friday-night class at the cooking school. She didn't have the energy.

So, instead, she shut the door behind her and trudged warily toward the silent Logan, tensed for whatever he wanted and whatever pressure he'd exert on her to get it. Would he suggest they go out for a drink or maybe a late movie? Although she wasn't in the mood to be social after a day as long as this one, she was also fresh out of the starch she needed to resist him.

As she drew closer, she could see he wasn't going to make it easy for her either. His soft-looking chambray shirt was unbuttoned to reveal a wide, tantalizing slice of his hard, wide chest. Gaze glued there, she hesitated again.

Tell him no, she reminded herself. *No way, no how—*

Well, she couldn't expect the impossible. *Just tell him "not tonight."*

Straightening her shoulders, she took a few resolute steps forward, then halted again when she suddenly realized exactly why he was so silent.

He wasn't lying in wait after all.

He was lying on the floor, sound asleep.

Bemused, Elena moved closer to stand over him. From this distance and with her vision more accustomed to the three-quarter darkness, she could clearly see that his thick eyelashes were fanned against the chiseled angle of his cheekbones. His face was relaxed, and though it didn't look any younger or less masculine in repose, Logan asleep appeared less…worrisome.

Without a qualm, she took the unprecedented opportunity to study him. What a secret pleasure it was, to look at him to her heart's content without fearing she was giving anything away.

She let her gaze wander past his closed eyes and

his straight, masculine nose to his so-interesting mouth. It was a wide mouth with full lips, that even in sleep seemed to be on the verge of smiling. An answering urge kicked up the edges of her own lips as she took in his square chin roughened by a hint of stubble. The whiskers there would glint like gold if the light was brighter.

His pulse beat steadily against his neck and she looked past it to the wedge of curling, dark-gold hair she could see between the spread edges of his open shirt. The fabric framed the heavy, masculine swells of his pectoral muscles and she stared at them, fascinated.

Heat sparked low in her belly then trickled downward. She thought she could see his heart beating too, pulsing against the skin at the center of his breastbone.

Without thinking, she bent toward it, wanting to put her mouth on it, her mouth on him, *there.*

His eyes still closed, Logan suddenly jerked, his arms flinging outward.

Gasping, she jumped back, but his hand still smacked her calf then settled onto her foot. With a half murmur, half groan, he settled back into sleep.

Elena sighed. He'd have plenty more to groan about if he spent any more time on the floor. She tapped her foot to jiggle his hand. ''Wake up.''

He didn't do anything but breathe more deeply. Sighing again, she hunkered down, making sure to tuck her knee-length black skirt under her behind, and shook his shoulder. ''Logan. Logan, time for bed.''

His eyes slowly opened, then even more slowly focused on her face. "Wuz I dreaming or'd you say 'time for bed'?"

She decided against answering. "Come on, big guy, get up."

His hand slid up her foot to circle her ankle. It felt hot against her sheer, nude-colored stockings. "Don't want to get up," he murmured, his lashes drifting down again. "Too tired."

She frowned. "Logan."

"Not moving," he answered, eyes still shut.

"You can't stay here all night."

He made an agreeable sound, but his muscles didn't shift.

"Logan..."

"Too tired," he murmured again. "Too tired to get up the stairs."

Shaking her head, she released another sigh. "Come on," she cajoled. "If you go upstairs you get a kiss good night."

One golden-brown eye creaked open. "From who?"

She grimaced. "Me, I suppose."

Dark lashes swept down. "Naah."

"For goodness sake," Elena spat out crossly, suddenly annoyed with him. Here she'd been almost afraid when she saw him, thinking he wanted her so badly. Now a promise of her kiss couldn't budge him!

She set her purse and tote bag on the floor and grabbed him under the arm. "You can thank me tomorrow." Then pulling, she half-rose.

"Whoa, whoa," he protested, but she threw her weight backward in order to haul him up. Just when it seemed as if she'd lose the battle and topple to the floor herself, he got to his feet.

"Persistent little thing, aren't you?" he grumbled, blinking sleepily and looking rumpled and ridiculously attractive. "Can't you leave a guy alone?"

Elena propped her hands on her hips and glared. She was going to smack him, she really was, because she'd come home exhausted, and yet now there was definite electricity pulsing through her veins. Blame it on the brief adrenaline rush when she'd thought to avoid him, or the surge of lust from the pleasure of looking at his sleeping form, or the punch of energy needed to move his much bigger body.

Whatever the cause or causes, it meant another sleepless night, her mind buzzing with thoughts of kissing him, touching him, finally *being* with him.

If she never experienced a good night's sleep again it was going to be all his fault. She flung her arm toward the stairs and pointed. "Just get moving, would you?"

He cast another grumpy look at her over his shoulder as he tramped up the steps. "Bad day at the office, dear?"

She ignored the comment by focusing on the way the tails of his shirt hugged the denim curving over his rear end as he mounted the second flight of stairs. He shouldn't have that smile and that dark-golden hair and such a great behind, too. Really, there was just so much to resent about him.

Her ire was at a nice bubble when he paused outside the door of her apartment. "Keep moving, you're the next door down." With one hand at the small of his back, she gave him a shove.

Now why wasn't she surprised that he turned around instead of going forward?

She once again set her belongings on the floor and crossed her arms over her chest. "What now?"

It was mostly dark up here, too, and she couldn't read the expression on his face. "I remember something about a kiss good night."

She rolled her eyes. "Some other time, Rip Van Winkle."

He leaned one shoulder against her door. "What's got you riled?"

"Never mind." To move him out of the way, she put her hands on his chest. Bad idea. His skin was hot, his chest hair crisp against her palms. She jerked them away. "Good night, Logan."

"My kiss." His voice still sounded sleepy, but there was a thread of amusement there too.

"Logan."

"Don't get so huffy, I'm too tired even to pucker up." He leaned forward and turned his cheek. "Right here, sweetheart, and then I'll trudge down to my apartment and fall right back to sleep."

While she, on the other hand, would be left awake and aching. Oh, no. She refused to be the lone lust-tortured tonight. "Whatever you say, Logan," she said sweetly.

Then she rose on tiptoe and put her mouth against

his cheek. She didn't pucker up either. Instead, she left her mouth open and soft, then used her tongue to trace a wet path across to his lips.

His head automatically turned to meet hers and then she planted a juicy, sensual kiss on him. Holding on to his shoulders, she tilted her head to improve the fit of their mouths. She thrust her tongue between his lips, over the slick surface of his teeth, then laid it along his tongue, rubbing hers against his like a kitten in search of a cuddle.

His hands shot out to clutch her waist as she kept up the heat and the intensity of the kiss. Her palms slid from his shoulders, down his shirt and then inward, returning to the bare skin of his chest. She drew the edges of his shirt apart, then pushed it off his shoulders. When the garment caught on his elbows, she fell back on her heels. It broke the mouth-to-mouth kiss and left her staring at the muscled swells of his pecs.

Surrendering to instinct, she brought her mouth to one firm curve and tasted that too.

He groaned, his fingers tightening on her flesh. Elena forced her mouth off him, forced herself to step back.

My work here is finished, she thought, trying to control the ragged seesaw of her breathing. "Have a nice rest," she said, proud of her casual, so-calm tone.

"Mmm." He was silent a moment, and then he yawned. Hugely. "See you tomorrow."

As he turned from her, she heard herself call his name.

"Can it wait?" he asked, still walking away. "I'm damn tired."

And she was so buzzed on the taste, the feel of him that it was as if she'd downed cups of pure caffeine. *Yet Logan was walking away.*

He'd yawned after that kiss!

Oh, she'd give him something he couldn't walk away from. Her pride injured, her sensual skills challenged, she pounced, determined to drag him back. Her hand only found fabric, though, his shirt pulling completely free of his body as he continued forward.

But then he halted, turned, looked at her. Thanks to the shadows, she had to imagine his eyebrow winging up, though she knew it was happening all the same. "Sweetheart—"

"Don't 'sweetheart' me." She leaped forward and this time her hand found his. She hauled him to her door, pushed his back against it, then grabbed his hair with both hands to pull his head down to hers.

He laughed, the sound alert, awake, and quite, quite satisfied.

"Unh!" She grunted in frustration and released his head with enough force to send it thunking against the door.

"Ow." He rubbed at the back of his head. "What was that for?"

"You make me so mad," she said through clenched teeth. "That I'm going to...to..."

He grinned, even in the darkness she could see his teeth, even and white. "This sounds interesting. You're going to what?"

He was teasing her. She *knew* that. But there was a roar in her ears that went quite well with the rush in her blood. Well, fine, but he was going to pay for both of the sensations.

Grabbing his wrist, she moved him away from the door and unlocked it. Then she pushed her purse and bag over the threshold, towed Logan inside after them, and finally shut the door with her foot.

The small lamp on the floor of the near-empty living room was glowing, but its light was only enough to warm the night-time shadows. She glowered at Logan, hoping that if he couldn't see her displeasure he would at least feel it. "You're going to pay."

"I've been counting on it."

Ooooh, he was still laughing at her. "You better be careful. There's no one to come to your rescue. Gabby's spending the night at a friend's."

"I know." The laughter was absorbed by a new, very male heaviness in his voice. "Why do you think I was downstairs? I didn't want to risk you getting by me tonight, not when we have a chance to be alone."

Elena swallowed, the fight inside her dying. When they had a chance to go to bed together, he meant. Both anticipation and nervousness rippled through her. "Oh, Logan."

He reached out to cup her cheek in his palm. "We don't have to. I really didn't mean to rush right into that—into it." His thumb caressed her mouth. "But this little feature packs a wallop when you want it to. I'm so horny I can't see straight."

"Logan…"

"Hell, I'm sorry to be crude." His laugh sounded a bit rueful now. "Maybe I *should* go along to my own apartment."

"Don't you dare," Elena heard herself say. And she was glad, so glad.

He was here, half-naked, and hers…at least for the night. Only an idiot would send him away now. Except—

"Do you…do you have a condom?" she whispered, feeling herself go hot all over.

Without a word, he slid both hands into the front pockets of his jeans to pull out a wealth of foil-wrapped packets.

A nervous giggle popped out of her mouth, even as her face went hotter. "So many?"

He leaned close, his voice low and sheepish. "The truth is, I didn't want my mother to find them. It's my entire stash."

She'd forgotten his mother! "Oh, Logan. Your mother—"

"Won't hear or know a thing. Her bedroom is on the opposite side of my apartment from the bedrooms in this one."

Elena hesitated. "I don't know. I'm not sure if I can forget—"

"Why don't you let me worry about that?" He stuffed the condoms away and drew her near his naked chest. One hand tilted up her chin and he brushed his mouth against hers. Back. Forth.

She shivered. "There's something else," she said against his mouth.

"Nothing." He hugged her, turning her cheek against his chest.

Elena couldn't help but shift her head to put her lips to his hot flesh. He smelled delicious, and she skimmed the tip of her nose over his chest, *mmm*ing in appreciation. There *was* something else, she thought vaguely. Something to think about, to tell him. Something she needed to do...?

Her head lifted, only to find his mouth waiting for hers. The kiss was gentle, a beginning, a slow exploration knowing that there was time for everything tonight.

Still, despite the pleasure running through her and the ratcheting level of desire in her blood, that last thought continued niggling at her.

"Logan—"

"Shh. Don't talk. Don't say another word." His mouth came down on hers, hard, deliberate, delirium-inducing.

Elena let him have her.

Chapter Nine

Logan didn't want Elena to say anything at all. Talking could lead to trouble. Talking could lead to stopping.

And if he was going to retain any shred of male dignity, he had to get her naked and get inside her. He'd manage foreplay—hell, he'd been fantasizing about foreplay with Elena for days, weeks, months—but he had to get on the straight track to satisfaction or else.

Or else this nice little case of lust he had going would transform into a roaring, howling beast he didn't know how to leash.

He didn't even know what to call the feeling, but Elena brought it to snarling life inside him.

Taming it the only way he knew how, by feeding

its hunger for Elena, Logan slid his tongue deeper into her mouth. At the same time, he pulled her shirt from the waistband of her skirt. His hands were shaking, his fingers like clumsy paws, but he managed to unfasten the tiny buttons marching up its front.

Her moan was soft and sweet when his palms skimmed her bare shoulders as he drew the shirt away. Needing to catch his breath, he lifted his head and looked down, only to lose all his air again. Wearing a short dark skirt and a lacy white bra that half bared the plump mounds of her breasts, Elena looked like a French maid fantasy come to life.

Standing in the dim room before him, her eyes were wide pools and her mouth was reddened and swollen from his kisses. She looked exotic, erotic, like every dark desire and every dark need he wanted to pretend wasn't inside a civilized man like himself.

That desire, that need, they were the beast, and as he looked at Elena it flexed its claws, digging deep, part-pleasure, part-pain.

"Take it off," he heard himself say in a harsh voice. He didn't trust himself to touch her right now.

"Logan..."

She was getting ready to talk again. He sucked in a quick breath, trying to keep control. "Take your bra off."

Then she smiled, secret, seductive, and it stroked the wildness inside of him. "All right." Her hand lifted to toy with the front clasp of her bra.

He couldn't look away. His focus narrowed to her slim, scarlet-tipped forefinger and the tiny circles it was making on the bra's fastening. A flick of her thumb and she would spill out of those lacy cups. A flick of her thumb and he could let her spill into his palms or into his mouth.

"Take it off," he whispered hoarsely.

Elena smiled again. "I will. Soon."

Fisting his hands at his sides, he shook his head. "Don't tease me."

She gave him a look through her sweep of lashes that said teasing was exactly what she wanted to do. Logan dug his nails into his palms, holding on, holding out against the need to touch, grab, take. Desire burned like hot breath over his skin as he tried to find an ounce of the urbanity that usually defined him.

She wouldn't recognize the man she made him into. He didn't recognize himself. But it was too late to pull back.

The electronic beep of a watch alarm penetrated his consciousness. Frowning, Elena stilled.

"Oh, no," she said, touching the watch on her wrist. "I *knew* there was something I had to tell you."

Blood pounded through his body. "Nothing's going to stop what's happening here."

"Just a postponement," she said breezily, then turned away.

"Elena!" He lunged for her, and missed, thank God, before he could scare the hell out of her and embarrass himself.

She bent over her tote bag that was sitting on the floor by the front door. Though Logan had stopped himself from grabbing her, he couldn't stop his gaze from climbing the length of the back of her thigh, the round curve of her butt. Then it dropped down the sweep of her spine and around to her breasts, their weight confined by the bra.

He wanted them free.

"Elena..."

She straightened and he tried to pretend what he saw in her hands wasn't there. But, hell, there was no denying that she was clasping that damn shoebox-crib that held her eggs-assignment.

"No." He shook his head. "Not tonight."

Her lips twitched as her eyes opened wide with innocence. "It takes just a few minutes to feed them and put them back to sleep."

The beast was clawing at him, demanding even louder to be released. "Unless you want a plate of scrambled eggs before sex, Elena, you will very, very carefully put that box somewhere safe and sound."

She smiled again, then tossed the box, not even looking to see where it landed.

Startled, he took an automatic step toward it himself.

"Don't bother," Elena called softly. "Gabby's babysitting for me tonight."

His gaze jerked back to her face. "Then the interruption—"

"Was payback." She made a big show of yawning, ending with a dainty pat of her hand over her mouth. "For that."

Payback. Teasing.

Torment.

She had no idea of the man or the mood she was playing with. It should have checked him, that naiveté, but instead it only goaded him further.

"No more games," he said flatly, holding out his hand. "Come here."

Elena stilled, a frown between her arched eyebrows. She looked apprehensive.

Good. Someone had to take care, and, after all these years, he knew it wouldn't be him. He'd avoided her, avoided this very situation, since she was sixteen years old. He'd sensed then the reckless wildness lurking inside him. The wildness only she seemed to bring alive.

Eleven years ago, it had scared the hell out of him and he'd not wanted to scare the hell out of *her*. But they were years older and way, way past the stopping point now.

"Come here."

Elena slowly moved toward him.

"It's all right," he reassured her. And it was, now that she was coming closer. He could keep the beast at bay as long as he had her near and as long as he knew he would have her soon.

When she was an arm's reach away, he was able to gently draw her close. The driving need inside him subsided from a roar to a purr and he reveled at the feel of her bare skin against his. He rested his cheek against the top of her head. "It's all right," he repeated, reassuring them both.

Then he edged her away and gently unfastened her bra. Without even looking at her breasts, he brought her back against his bare chest and drew the under-garment away.

She shivered.

He closed his eyes, savoring the smooth heat of her skin and the soft poke of her hardened nipples against his chest. His hands ran down her back, soothing, soothing, as the exotic scent of sun-soaked flowers rose off her flesh.

With the prize of her naked skin and her perfumed scent, the beast inside him quieted. Logan tugged on the ends of Elena's hair to coax her head back and he kissed her again. Gentle too, but thorough, his tongue exploring the undersides of her lips, then moving in to sweep across her own tongue.

Elena made small sounds at the back of her throat and moved her body restlessly, her tight nipples rubbing against his chest. Logan's body went harder, but her obvious, growing excitement gave him the power to keep his own desires in check.

If he took Elena *out* of control, he thought, he could keep himself *under* control.

He broke the kiss only to rain kisses down her throat. She bowed in his arms and he took the invitation for what it was—he feasted on her breasts.

But slowly there, too. First licking around them, and under them, tickling the crease beneath the plump curves with little flicks of his tongue. Elena clutched his head with her hands, and when her nails bit into his scalp he let his mouth move to her nipple and suck it inside.

Her body shuddered. He held her, his thumbs under

her breasts, his fingers splayed across her back and brought her to his mouth at his will. He was greedy in his enjoyment of her, sucking slow and gentle, then increasing the pressure to draw as much of her into his mouth as he could.

Edging away, he paused to admire. She looked dazed, her eyes half-open but almost all pupil. Her fast breaths caused her breasts to rise and fall, rise and fall, the tips berry-red and wet from his mouth.

"Please, Logan," she whispered.

He smiled, still calm because she wasn't, and slid his thumbs up the curves of her lower breasts to brush over the distended nipples, back and forth. "Please what, honey?" Back and forth again.

She slid her hands from his waist to his chest. His erection ached as she inched her way along his skin. "Just...please." The pads of her thumbs stroked across his own hard nipples.

He jerked. Her gaze on his face, she stroked again. Calmness fled.

"Enough." He didn't recognize his own voice, but he recognized the impetus—the beast—that spurred him to lift her into his arms. "Time for bed."

"Futon." A little smile tugged the corners of her lips. "I left the bed back at my house and only have a futon here."

Bed, futon, countertop, card table. It didn't matter what the surface was, as long as it was horizontal. He strode down the three-door hallway and shoved a door open with his foot.

"Gabby's room."

Groaning aloud, he spun and used his shoulder to push open the door across the hall. The room was dark, a slice of moonlight the only illumination. The full-size futon was positioned left-center. Logan felt a brief pang of regret at the thought of his king-size mattress and box springs, but then he breathed in, he breathed in the scent of Elena that filled the room, and nothing else mattered but her.

He needed to touch her, get close to her, rub himself in her essence. It was an instinct, an obsession, the beast reasserting itself again, and Logan's hands shook with its influence as he laid her down on her back. He immediately knelt beside her, determined to have her naked. Now.

She helped. It was as if she needed herself bared to him. In moments she was lying on the sheets covering the futon, her body uncovered.

Her body his.

Logan felt her hands at the buttons of his jeans and he brushed them away. "Not yet."

The moonlight lent a silver edge to her creamy curves. Her navel was a shadowed, sexy dimple. He leaned over to test it with his tongue. She flinched, and he held her still with his palm flattened against her lower belly.

He tongued her navel again, the shallow penetration satisfying only in that it was another taste of Elena. She moaned and he praised the sound by edging his pinky into the curling hair at the V of her thighs.

The scent of hot flowers rose around him.

He felt her hand at his waistband again, and again he impatiently brushed it away. Didn't she understand? The only way to subdue the clamoring, ravenous need inside him was to give it little tastes of her at a time.

He took another, running his mouth down her thighs then shifting to gently bite the skin over her knee. She reacted perfectly, moaning with pleasure even as she instinctively edged away from the strange touch by drawing her knee up and out.

He did the same with the other knee.

And so did she.

Her open knees also opened her thighs. He stroked his palms up the insides of them, toward the tantalizing place that was his.

His. It was that thought that kept him sane and that kept his caresses gentle and unhurried.

He drew his forefinger lightly over the soft, wet cleft.

"Logan." His name was a plea, a very sexy demand.

"Mmm." He drew his finger down.

"Let me touch you." She tried to sit up, but he pushed her back down, afraid of what might happen if she took what she wanted.

His finger drew up, drew down. She opened for him, her body inviting his deeper touch. He slid inside.

She cried out.

He drew out the finger, then slid two inside.

"Logan."

"Shh. This is so good," he told her, his voice hoarse. "This is what I need."

Her head moved back and forth against the pillow. "No. It's what I need."

"Same thing, honey. Same thing." His hand took her slowly, it took in order to feed his desire and to feed hers.

His body throbbed with heat, demanding release, but it was all right because his hand was slick with Elena, slick with her arousal, slick with the evidence that he wasn't the only one at the mercy of sex.

"Don't," she whispered. "Don't."

"Don't what?"

"Not like this."

He froze. *She wants me to stop?* But then he realized her hands were at the buttons of his jeans again. She wanted them both naked. She wanted to make love with him. He remembered promising to give to her, that she could take from *him,* and so he tore open his pants and shoved himself free of the rest of his clothing.

Then he dropped between her thighs.

The wet heat at the center of her body kissed his arousal, and he gritted his teeth against the beast's instant need to dive inside. Instead he lightly, slowly caressed her there with himself.

Her eyes closed and she writhed, then lifted herself up to him. "*No peudo pensar.* I can't think."

"You're not supposed to think," he whispered against her ear. "You're supposed to feel. Feel me, Elena." He rubbed against her once more.

Her fingers clutched his head and she brought his lips to hers, her mouth greedy on his. "Now," she said against his lips. "I want it now."

Again, her demanding excitement helped him restrain his. Shaking his head, he rolled off her to lie stomach-down beside her on the futon. "Not so soon."

Her lower lip pushed out—an expression he would dare to call a pout if the woman was anyone but Elena. "I've been waiting forever," she complained.

He laughed softly, pleased by the truculence in her voice.

She narrowed her eyes. "You're making fun of me."

"Not in a million years." With his hip grazing hers, he was close enough, and she was obviously aroused enough, that the savageness inside him stayed at a simmer. He leaned over to kiss her softly, his hand cupping and fondling her breast.

But with the touch, the kiss, he seduced himself and he was compelled to firm his touch, to take the kiss deeper. Elena's hand came around the back of his head, and he felt her breast swell in his hand.

A sharp, hot shudder worked its way down his back. He groaned, it was all so damn, damn good, and then she clutched his shoulders, pushed, shoving him flat to the futon so he was beneath her.

"Elena, no," he choked out.

"Logan, yes," she whispered back. The ends of her hair swept across his cheek as she drew her hot little mouth over his chin and then down his neck to his chest. She kissed him, then added little half bites that should have been almost sweet, but that in his highly aroused state were too little, too light, too *not enough.*

He palmed the back of her head to press her harder against his flesh, but she twisted away and sat up. Her soft laughter echoed in the near-empty room.

He reached for her.

She edged back. "Nuh-uh-uh." She shook her finger at him, mischief tilting up the corners of her eyes. "Not so soon."

Deep inside him, the wildness was rising again. He closed his eyes, reaching for the control to hold it back.

It was why he missed that dangerous move of her hand.

Small fingers slid over his erection.

He jerked up, she pushed him down with her free hand, running her other over him again. "No, Elena, no," he said.

She glanced at his face, then gazed back down at what she held in a gentle fist. *"Eres mio."*

"Yes." He had no idea what she'd said, but it didn't matter. "Now stop."

"Mine." She caressed the length of him with her hand. Logan tensed, trying desperately to remember he was a sophisticated, mature man.

Then she lightly squeezed.

Sophistication shattered.

In the instant it took for the heat to sweep across his body, his brain, he reversed their positions again.

But this time when he came between her thighs he wasn't going to tease or caress or stop.

She must have seen it on his face. Her palms pushed against his chest as he lowered to her. "Logan—"

"Playtime's over, honey."

"Condom."

Condom? For a moment he thought she was speaking in Spanish again because he didn't recognize the word. It made no sense to the wildness riding him. Then he cursed and cursed again as he groped for his jeans.

As his hands came up empty, an image burst in his mind, beautiful and pure. Elena, her breasts ripe and full, her belly round with his child. Elena pregnant with their baby.

The idea should scare him soft, but instead his lust surged, his body going even harder. He spat out another curse.

"I believe that's what I'm waiting for," Elena said, a hint of laughter in her voice. She dangled a foil-wrapped square in front of his face. "Will this help?"

He snatched it out of her hand. "I wouldn't laugh if I were you," he said hoarsely, as he took care of the condom then positioned himself between her thighs again.

"Why—" The word ended on a gasp as he entered her in one long stroke.

He groaned, holding himself still and deep. "Elena. You're so tight. You…" His mind scrambled, trying to figure out how she could have seemed so slick and ready, yet now appeared in near...pain. Her body squeezed down on his, hard.

"Elena. Honey." He dropped his forehead against hers. "Are you all right?"

She nodded once, but her gaze slid away.

He swallowed. "Honey, I can't pull out without hurting you more. Not unless you relax, okay? Relax your muscles, the ones inside. Do you know what I mean?"

She nodded, but didn't move, outside or in.

He brushed her hair off her face, then kissed her forehead. "I know I hurt you. I hate myself for it. But as soon as you ease up a little, I'll be able to move off you."

She nodded again, but again nothing happened. A tear dripped down her cheek. "I...I can't," she whispered.

The beast, he noted thankfully, had retreated to its lair. Only tenderness entwined with his desire as Logan kissed the next tear away. "Let me help you, honey."

He eased his body a little off hers and reached down between them with one hand. She jumped—her inner muscles clenching tighter—when he found the knot of nerves within her silky folds. "Shh," he soothed, and stroked it gently, light circles that he hoped would distract her.

He ran his mouth over each of her eyes, soaking up the tears and then he moved to her lips again, kissing her gently even as he kept touching, touching, touching her.

He felt her inner muscles ease a little even as a new tension entered her body. Her tongue met his and he stroked past it, stroking deeply with the same rhythm as his fingers.

Her body softened and opened around his invasion. He could move within her now and he slowly began to draw out. She tore her mouth from his. "Logan?"

"Don't worry. I'm not going to hurt you again."

"You're *leaving* me?" Her hands clamped down on his hips. "You better not be leaving me."

He froze. "Elena. Maybe we should talk. Maybe—"

His words were cut off as she lifted her hips and took him back inside her. "Maybe we should finish this," she said, her expression stubborn.

He closed his eyes. How many times was a man supposed to say "no" to a woman as beautiful and arousing as this? Wasn't once enough?

"On one condition," he said, opening his eyes to look down into hers. He could tell she was determined to see this through, but he'd be damned if it was for all the wrong reasons when only one counted…desire.

Her eyes narrowed suspiciously. "What condition?"

He sighed. She was going to make things difficult for him until the end of his life, he could tell. "We're not going to do this for your pride, my ego or any other stupid reason like our long-ago past. Agreed?"

"Agreed. But—"

He cut her off with another kiss and then when he had her quiet, he rolled, bringing her on top of him.

She instinctively sat up, winced, then minutely adjusted her position with a little shimmy of her hips.

He groaned.

She looked down at him, her eyes glinting with satisfaction. "You like that." She shimmied again.

Reaching out, he rediscovered her small knot of nerves, strummed it with his thumb. Her gasp was all pleasure this time. "And you like that," he countered.

He pushed up with his body and she lifted. She lowered when he did. He caressed her hip. "That's right, honey. Move just like that."

Her nostrils flared as she caught the rhythm.

His thumb strummed over her flesh again. "And I'll move just like this."

Elena danced over him, her movements graceful, erotic. With his free hand, he caught her nipple between his thumb and fingers. Her head dropped bonelessly back as she rode him and the building pleasure.

He watched her closely, her coiling tension communicating itself through her tightening body. She rose up one more time, slid slowly down and then it happened.

Her hips ground against his and his fingers plucked just that much harder. She shuddered wildly. He meant to watch it all the way through, he meant to make sure he saw her wring every atom of satisfaction from the event, but then her inner muscles clenched down on him again—tight, tighter.

"Elena." He groaned and lifted himself up, pushing into her, pushing into her body, invading her climax and giving her his.

She fell against him, and for several minutes they lay plastered together, both of them occasionally shivering with aftershocks of pleasure.

It was only after he'd forced himself up to dispose of the condom then returned to the futon and Elena's arms that she finally spoke. *"Te idio,"* she said, then she turned her cheek against his chest and bit him.

"Ow!" He grabbed a handful of her hair and lifted her head to meet her gaze. "What was that?"

Her expression was smug. "I said, I hate you. The bite is self-explanatory."

"Like hell it is. I'm sorry I hurt you, but—"

She bit him again. "Shut up."

He rubbed his abused flesh. "You confuse me."

"My goal in life," she said flippantly.

He sighed, then put his arms around her and shifted them both so they were face-to-face on one pillow. "I suppose it would be too much to ask for you to drift off into a nice, quiet, post-coital sleep."

"I thought that was the guy's job."

Logan sighed again. This sassiness was not a good sign. Elena was up to her old tricks, erecting prickly barriers between them, even after they'd been as intimate as two people could get.

As intimate as she'd ever been with any man.

"You were a virgin."

"That's why I said I hate you," she said, half smiling even as her gaze drifted away from his. "Look at what I've been missing out on. I could have had *years* of pleasure!"

He saw red. He closed his eyes against the color

of angry, instant temper, but it was still there, pulsing behind his eyelids. "I don't know if I'm madder at the idea of you wishing I'd seduced you at sixteen or at the idea of you being pleasured by a succession of other men."

"I'm sorry."

Her apology had him opening his eyes, instantly suspicious. "What did you say?" he asked.

She bit her lip, then ran her hand through his hair. "That was a nasty crack." She toyed with one lock, curling it around her finger. "I…I don't know what I wish, but I understand why you said no that night."

Logan wasn't sure even *he* knew all the answers to that, but he nodded then took the opportunity to broach another subject. "You've waited a long time to…to…"

"Have sex?" she prompted.

He didn't know why the two simple words made him want to tear something into a thousand little pieces. "Make love."

Her shoulder jerked in a partial shrug. "Not any particular reason. I just never found the right man at the right time."

She'd never trusted a man that much, Logan realized, gathering her closer. Elena was so very careful with sharing herself, soul *and* body. But for a little time, anyway, she'd trusted him.

She yawned and closed her eyes, snuggling her cheek into the pillow.

"What are you doing now?" he asked. Besides avoiding him, because that was perfectly obvious.

"Mmm," she murmured, wriggling within his embrace as if trying to get more comfortable. "Settling into that nice, quiet, post-coital sleep you requested."

He let her wriggle and he let her close her eyes, but he didn't let her out of his arms. His gaze on her face, he reran the entire act in his mind. Once he'd entered her and realized how inexperienced she was, that wildness she called from him had stayed safely in the distance. He didn't know if he could have handled being at the mercy of the beast this first time with her.

She made a little sound and he could tell she actually *was* settling into sleep now. He leaned forward and kissed the tip of her nose, then drew in a long breath that was an unforgettable combination of Elena's sun-washed-flowers scent and sex.

Some time before dawn, Logan rose from the futon, remembering Elena's concern that his mother would know they'd slept together. He softly kissed Elena's mouth and whispered that he'd see her later. She murmured in response, her hand lifting drowsily to touch his cheek.

His body instantly hardened and he felt the stirrings of rampant lust reawakening. He had to force himself away from her because he wanted with equal strength both to take her again and to tenderly to guard her sleep.

It was a toss-up, really, as to which impulse was more dangerous. Either way he was at the mercy of the beast…or at the mercy of the most surprising, sexy, staggeringly beautiful woman he'd ever known.

Chapter Ten

Logan tripped over the hammer he'd left on the floor and saved himself from falling by shoving his hand against the downstairs kitchen doorjamb—jamming a thick splinter into the heel of his thumb at the same time.

"Damn this entire day to hell," he muttered, staring down at his wounded palm. The shard of wood had worked itself deep.

He hated splinters. He hated digging them out. He hated that this day had gone sour from the early-morning moment when he'd left Elena's bed.

His mother came around the corner, apparently just in from her afternoon shift at the thrift shop that supported the nearby children's hospital. "Was that you I heard cursing?"

"Guilty." Logan scowled at his hand again. Then he looked back at his mother, trying to sound polite. "How was your day?"

"Oh, fine," she said with a vague smile.

Laura Chase was continuing with her usual Saturday schedule, just as the other women in Logan's life were continuing with theirs. Gabby had been in and out but was now in, working on a school project, she'd said. Elena had left the house in the morning, sneaking out in an effort to avoid him, Logan was sure. He'd called her office to no avail and Gabby had no idea when to expect her.

Logan had no idea what to expect *from* her, but that she'd ducked out without talking to him was a very bad sign that had made for a very bad day.

"Do you have plans for dinner?" his mother asked. "Or would you like me to cook for you?"

Logan stifled a groan. There had been help in the Chase kitchen for his mother's forty-plus years of marriage and so her culinary talents hadn't developed past the green Jell-O salads and tuna-and-potato chip casseroles that must have been standard home-ec class fare when she was a young woman. "Maybe we can call for carry-out," he suggested, then hesitated. "If you're still here, that is."

Her silver-blond eyebrows rose. "Why wouldn't I be?"

He cleared his throat. "I thought maybe you would be going back home today."

She shook her head. "Not yet."

Logan sighed, a headache starting to pulse at his

temples in time with the splinter in his hand. "Mom, what the heck are you doing here?"

She looked down at her hands, twisting her wedding set around and around. "I'm trying to get your father's attention."

"I think you have that. He's phoned you every night, but you refuse to take his calls."

"I need to shake him up a little more. Like you did."

"Like *I* did?"

She nodded. "When you left the family company you really threw your father for a loop."

Logan grimaced again, regretting having started the conversation. "Mom, I'm sor—"

"Don't be sorry. I'm proud of you for taking charge of your life. You shouldn't wait as long as I have to get what you want."

Logan grimaced again. "I didn't realize you've been so unhappy."

"Oh, don't get me wrong. I've been quite content letting Jonathon have his way for many of the years we've been married. He's a fascinating, challenging man, Logan, and I've enjoyed quietly supporting him as he's built the business. But once Griffin came back to Strawberry Bay, and especially now that he's married, I expected your father to give more of the responsibility to him. I want Jonathon to start making some plans to ease up, if not retire altogether. But he won't listen to me."

"Mom, he's never listened to anyone."

Her laugh sounded a little bit sad. "You're right.

But I think it's because none of us have demanded he hear us. We've let him have his own way for too, too long.''

But his father was more stubborn than any person he'd ever met—save one. "I hope you know what you're doing.''

She half smiled. "Me, too.'' Then she turned to make her way upstairs.

Logan started poking at his sliver, now welcoming the distraction. At least this was an issue—unlike his parents' marriage, unlike his murky relationship with Elena—with a clear-cut solution.

About three hours later, the two solution-hazy problems arrived at the Victorian together. Logan was in the parlor, scraping the last of the wallpaper layers when the front door opened and Elena arrived, Jonathon Chase in her wake.

Her footsteps faltered when she caught sight of Logan. "Oh. Hi." Her gaze bounced off his face to settle somewhere in the vicinity of his left shoulder.

"Hi." He crossed his arms over his chest, his temper only needing her obvious discomfort to start burning. "Seven voice-mail messages I left you. Didn't you get one of them?''

"Uh...well, I've had a very busy day.''

Damn this awkwardness! If she hadn't escaped this morning without talking to him, if she had returned just *one* of his phone calls, he could have prevented this. But no, she'd done her best to avoid him and avoid giving them a chance to establish some sort of new order after their intimacy.

"We need to talk," he said through his teeth.

Elena swallowed, then nodded toward his father. "But Mr. Chase, I mean, your, um, your father's here."

Jonathon adjusted the knot of his silver-and-black tie. "I'm here to see Laura."

"Oh!" Elena said brightly. "Why don't I take you up to her?"

Before Logan could protest, she was linking her arm with his father's and towing him up the stairs with her, chattering all the way. Shaking his head, Logan lounged against the wall and watched the little sneak ride off.

But no, no way, was she going into the sunset without him. Not until he made sure she didn't think they'd had a one-night stand, which was just what a woman as stubbornly wary as Elena *would* think. Tamping down his frustration, he slowly headed after them.

The scene in the upstairs hallway did nothing to improve his mood. Elena had disappeared—presumably she'd already scurried into her apartment. Logan's headache returned to pound at his temples.

Knowing her, she'd probably refuse to let him in.

Just as his mother was refusing his father. Because Jonathon Chase was having ill luck with his woman too. As Logan watched, his father continued banging on Logan's apartment door with his palm.

"Laura, for God's sake, open up!"

Logan couldn't hear the precise words of his mother's muffled response, but judging from his father's expression, it wasn't what Jonathon had wanted to hear. Unsure exactly what to do, Logan halted, standing between the two apartments. The older man turned his glare from the door to his son.

"Your mother is acting foolishly," he said.

"Uh, well…"

"We have a dinner at the club tonight," Jonathon said, his expression thunderous. "A *business* dinner."

"Maybe Mom's tired of business dinners," Logan ventured. "You might want to—"

"I don't have time for this," Jonathon said over him. "Unlock the door for me, Logan."

Logan automatically shoved his hand in his pocket, but when his fingers encountered metal, he hesitated. "Sorry, Dad." He shrugged. "I left my set of keys inside."

Jonathon's frown deepened. He banged on the door again. "Laura. Laura, we have the Redwells—George and Tanya—at 7:00!"

When there was no response, he muttered to himself and looked down at his watch. Then his head slowly came up and the gleam in his eye was speculative. "*You* could come with me, Logan."

He rolled his eyes. "Dad, forget the Redwells. Mom has moved out. Do you grasp that?"

His father waved a hand. "We'll work through it. But George Redwell has always had a soft spot for you. With your help I can nail him down on that new contract."

Logan inhaled a long breath. "I don't work for Chase Electronics anymore, Dad, remember?"

His father made another dismissive gesture with his hand. "Haven't you played tinker toys long enough? Come on, son. What you're doing here isn't important. Let's go out to dinner, talk real business, and—"

"Logan?" Suddenly, Elena's door was flung open and she poked her head out. "Could you come in here, please?"

Surprised, he merely stared at her for a moment. He'd thought nothing short of another earthquake in Strawberry Bay would shake her out of that apartment for a face-to-face with him.

"Logan?" Her face was flushed but her gaze rested squarely on his face.

"About dinner—" his father started.

"Sorry, Dad—" Logan grinned as Jonathon started to sputter "—but Beauty calls." He was inside Elena's apartment before the old man could manage another word.

Logan shut the door behind him, then strode directly to Elena and took her face between his hands. He laid a smacking kiss on her lips. "Thank you for that."

She broke away from him. "Thank Gabby," she said, avoiding his eyes again. "She heard a commotion in the hall."

Gabby was doing homework at the card table and smiled when Logan walked over and bent down to kiss her loudly on top of the head. "Thank you, Gabby."

She caught his hand for a moment. "She's full of baloney," she whispered to him. "We both heard the commotion, and she couldn't get to the door fast enough. By the way, though, what you've done with this place *is* important.''

He stilled, looking back at her. This time he noticed Gabby wasn't doing schoolwork after all, but was instead sketching in a spiral-bound pad. Her subject was Elena again, caught staring off into space, her usual energy and take-me-or-leave-me attitude absent. It was Elena quiet, her mouth soft, her eyes almost...yearning.

He glanced at the stiff shoulders and straight spine of the real-life Elena, standing with her back toward him as she rummaged through her tote bag. Then he again studied the drawing that revealed a so-much-more vulnerable woman.

It was Elena through Gabby's—an artist's—eye, an eye that saw beneath the layers. It was the same kind of vision that he had for this house and others like it. His eyes pierced the shell built up over the years to see the true beauty beneath.

''Yeah,'' he said, smiling at Gabby. ''I know. It's important.''

As was this moment with Elena. He strolled over to her, then took her shoulders to spin her toward him. ''I didn't get the chance for a proper hello.''

When she instantly backed up, he let her go, stung by another rejection. Hell, what was the point, he thought, frustrated again as he studied her beautiful, but suspicious face. Maybe there was no good reason to pursue this. She was too wary, too much work.

He glanced away, his eye catching on Gabby's

sketch. Suddenly a dozen memories of the night before swamped him: The velvety skin of the concave curve of Elena's belly, the sound of her breathy moans, the feel of her shuddering against his hands.

He'd buried those memories with the irritation and frustration he'd felt when she'd left without seeing him that morning. He'd been letting her tough shell get in the way of remembering how good it had been with her last night. But Gabby's sketch reminded him that Elena was more, much more, than the thorny protection she wore.

Calmer now, Logan smiled at her. So what that she'd been busy reconstructing all her barriers? Last night he'd uncovered her sweetness and fire and, by God, he could do it again.

Elena wanted to order Logan out of her apartment. But since he owned it, and since the only rent she was paying was the temporary custody of one ridiculous painting, she settled for screaming instead.

She did that in the bathroom, muffling the sound by holding a thick bath towel against her face. Then she wet a washcloth with cold water and bathed the back of her neck and her wrists.

Cool, she thought to herself as she left the bathroom. *Be cool.* Logan couldn't know he'd shattered her defenses the night before. He couldn't know how close he was to breaking into her heart. Given that kind of advantage, he might actually do the deed, and this time she wouldn't survive it.

She exited the bathroom to find him in the kitchen,

surrounded by the makings of a green salad. He was wearing a paint-stained pair of jeans, a T-shirt and a pair of heavy workboots. Looking up, he smiled at her, and she had to lock her knees to keep upright. The appeal of the combination of his country-club looks and construction-worker attire was even more difficult to ignore now.

Now that he'd made—had sex with her.

Elena took a deep breath and ignored the fact that he appeared to be settling in for the evening. She saw the carry-out menu from Gabby's favorite Italian place lying beside the phone. "You can't get into your own apartment yet?"

"Well, my dad's definitely gone from the house, but I'm still locked out," he said cheerfully. "Problem is, I think Mom left after Dad did. I've knocked and knocked, I tried calling my phone. No answer."

Elena closed her eyes. "You don't keep a spare key anywhere?"

"Oh, sure."

Her heart leaped. She could get rid of him now! "Where—?"

"It's the one my mother's using."

A strangled sound erupted from her throat.

He looked over. "What was that?"

It was a half-strangled scream. "Nothing," she lied. "Not a thing."

"Good. Gabby and I ordered pizza."

Elena sighed. He *was* settling in for the evening. The atmosphere in the apartment had been strained enough since the blow-up with Gabby the week before without adding Logan to the mix.

"As a matter of fact," Logan continued, "she went to pick it up. Which gives you and me a chance to talk."

Cool, Elena's mental voice cautioned again. "Sure." She forced herself to meet his gaze.

It was warm and golden and reminded her of how she'd felt last night as he caressed and kissed her. She'd tried so hard to act composed and sophisticated then, too, but her attempts at mastering the situation by teasing him had been completely overwhelmed by *his* teasing—teasing touches and teasing tastes. She hadn't stood a chance against him or the sexuality he so easily aroused in her.

He turned to lean against the counter and smile at her slowly, as if he could read her mind and approved the direction of her thoughts. "How are you today?"

"Fine," she said off-handedly, cool and casual. "Of course I'm fine. Why wouldn't I be fine? Aren't you fine? Is there a reason—"

Too late, she clamped her mouth shut on the decidedly *not* composed, *not* casual babble that was erupting from the deep well of awkwardness inside her. She whirled toward the refrigerator. "Can I get you something? Soda, iced tea, sex maybe, or…or…"

Hearing herself, she froze, mortified. Then she thunked her forehead a couple of times against the slick refrigerator door.

"Elena—"

She halted him with a violent wave of her hand. "If you laugh at me, you'll scar me for life. Better yet, I'll scar *you* for life."

He really did laugh now. "Good to see you're still in fighting form, honey."

Honey. He'd called her that last night, too. And she'd felt so honey-hot inside, everything all melty and sweet. Dangerously vulnerable. Desperate, she wrenched open the refrigerator and grabbed the first cold can, popped it open, drank.

Feeling slightly less ridiculous, she took another long swallow and then managed to turn and brave Logan again. With a pretend fascination, she studied the shoulder seam of his T-shirt.

It was much safer than his face.

"I don't mean to make you nervous," he said quietly.

"I'm not nervous." Always deny. Standing tall, she forced her gaze to his. "I've yet to meet a man who makes me nervous."

"Liar," he said, stepping close to her.

He lifted her chin with his hand and she refused to give him the satisfaction of retreating from the touch. "Though why I'd make you nervous *now* is something of a mystery." His grin was both devilish and gentle.

How the heck did he do that? It was just like that country-club construction-worker thing, Elena thought helplessly, a paradox created to unbalance a woman. To make her melt.

"After all," he continued, the grin growing. "I've

already had my wicked way with you." He leaned down as if to kiss her.

She surrendered to self-protective impulse and jerked away. It was time to get on with the plan she'd been preparing since waking up this morning. The plan she'd developed in case he seemed inclined to pursue their relationship. She had to protect herself, after all.

"What do you want, Logan?" she said matter-of-factly.

He blinked. "What do I want?"

The graceless gesture she made sent a slurp of soda splashing to the counter. She ignored it and calmly pinned him with her gaze. "Now that you've had your 'wicked way' as you put it, why are you here and what do you want? What do you want with me?"

He frowned, his eyes wary. "I'm not following you, Elena."

"You've had me. You said it yourself, and you're right. We did it. It's done. The fat lady sang. The party's over." She knew she was starting to babble again but somewhere in all these words she might find the right ones to send him away for good. "Eleven years of anticipation are finally over. Potential realized. The itch scratched, right?"

He hissed out a breath. "You're trying pretty hard to make me angry."

Pretty hard? She was trying with everything she had. "It's what you wanted, right? What I agreed to. 'Finish it once and for all,' you said. Well, we accomplished that last night."

"We accomplished that," he repeated in a low, flat voice.

She swallowed. It was so crucially important to be the first one to make the inevitable break. "Yes. Last night we ended, you know.... We ended us."

The gold of Logan's eyes was hard, now. Hard and hot. His mouth looked hard too. "How—why do you do this to me?" he finally bit out.

"I don't know what you mean." She clutched her soda can, reminding herself to play it cool and calm.

"I consider myself a good-natured, easygoing type of guy." A muscle ticked in his jaw. She thought she saw his hands shaking before he shoved them in his pockets as if he needed to restrain them. "Most people would agree with me."

She lifted one shoulder. "Yeah, you're a real Mr. Congeniality."

His nostrils flared. "You should be careful, honey."

"Oh, you think so?" She arched an eyebrow, even as her heartbeat jumped. But she was just inches away from getting his disturbing presence out of her life, she could feel it. If there was one thing she was good at, it was pushing men away before they got a chance to push *her* away. "I'm shaking in my shoes, Logan."

"Damn it." His hands whipped out, grabbed her by the shoulders, jerked her against him. "You infuriate me."

He'd pulled her onto her toes and she could feel his heart slamming against hers. His heartbeat was fast too, and though his hands on her were gentle, she decided against struggling. "Then let me go," she suggested, her mouth dry. Did it sound as if she was pleading? "Let's go our separate ways."

That muscle in his jaw ticking again, his eyes closed. After a moment he opened them to glare down at her. "Is that what you want?" he asked roughly.

"I..." All she had to say was yes! She knew it. One word and she would be safe again. "It's what will happen anyway," she heard herself whisper.

He opened his mouth, closed it, then he shook his head again. And then shook it some more.

"Damn you," he repeated, though this time he said it softly, the expression in his eyes more bemused than angry. "Up, down, in, out. You just can't be satisfied with one direction, can you? You've got to take me in all of them at once."

He pulled her closer and she found herself in his total embrace now, his arms around her, her cheek pressed against his chest. The embrace, the slowing rhythm of his heart, neither was a good sign, she thought in panic.

Worse, she wasn't doing anything to extricate herself.

He kissed the top of her head. "You know, I like things to be simple. Straightforward. Non-confrontational."

Elena nodded, which caused her cheek to rub against his chest. Oh, well. "Me too."

He laughed. "You don't have a simple, straightforward, non-confrontational cell in your whole body."

Elena suppressed a little smile. How could she resist him? "Is that a compliment?"

He laughed again, and inched her away to look down at her face. Then he sighed. "Has anyone ever told you you're mind-blowing beautiful?"

She bit her bottom lip.

"Of course they have." Logan rolled his eyes. "You make me mad, not stupid."

"Logan—"

"Shh." Framing her face with his hands, he leaned down and touched her lips with his.

Elena felt a wash of that traitorous, honey-hot melting. "Logan..."

"Shh." He kissed her again, just as lightly. "One night with you was not enough for me, do you understand? The party is *not* over, the fat lady has an entire Wagner opera left to sing, and the itch is definitely still driving me to distraction."

He was not helping. "But Logan—"

"Don't you deserve some pleasure?" He tapped her nose with one long finger. "I can promise that, I think."

Pleasure was one thing, she thought desperately, but there was that inevitable pain to follow it. "I don't have time for a...a..."

"A boyfriend?" His smile could charm her heart out of her chest. Hadn't it already worked with the pants off her body? "I think we're too old for that, don't you? But Elena, honey, I could be your lover."

"Maybe I don't have time for one of those, either," she said, but she was already so darn soft and he was so right about the pleasure. So much pleasure. When was the last time she'd indulged herself with anything that felt so good?

"You let me worry about your time." This kiss was long and demanding and told her that he already knew she'd surrendered. "You let me worry about that."

Chapter Eleven

Logan had never been a moody man. Just as he'd told Elena, he'd always been an even-tempered, good-natured, glass-half-full type of guy.

Those thoughts only made him swing the sledgehammer he was holding in both fists with more force. He hadn't planned on gutting so soon the tiny downstairs bathroom that had been added in the 1950s then redecorated in the 1970s, but yesterday, hitting something had become an imperative. The bubblegum-pink tile liberally embellished with stuck-on fluorescent flowers and peace signs made a perfect target.

Tile shattered and fell at his feet. He smiled at it grimly, swung again.

Elena had told him over a week ago that she didn't have time for him. Damn her, she'd been right.

A woman with nothing less than two jobs, a night class, a sister to raise and volunteer duties for the upcoming senior prom apparently didn't have time to sleep either. He didn't think she'd been to bed in three days.

She'd certainly not been in *his* bed.

The night after they'd first made love, he'd managed to talk her out of immediately ending this…this…this *thing* between them and talk himself into her bed for some very quiet and tender lovemaking after Gabby was safely asleep. He'd promised her pleasure and holding firmly to the beast's leash, he'd managed to make good on it.

But he'd seen her only five times since. Kissed her twice. Hell, he spent more time with his *mother* than he did with his lover.

Pitiful. He swung the sledgehammer again.

Compounding that, he had the feeling that Elena was relieved to be so busy. Oh, she claimed to be sorry she couldn't see him, but he saw the wariness that lingered in her eyes and in her voice and he knew that she was more comfortable blocking him than being with him.

It irritated him. A feeling which went perfectly with his sexual frustration. Not to mention the resentment he felt at how she so carefully maintained her emotional distance too. He'd told her weeks ago that he wanted to know her, but she continued ducking every personal question he posed.

A movement in the hall outside the bathroom caught his eye. Elena. He instantly tossed down the sledgehammer and leaped over the threshold to nab her.

She accepted his kiss, her mouth softening, but then she pushed away, laughing. "Hey, hey, hey. A woman needs to breathe now and again."

He pulled her back. "Not as much as I need this." He drew her onto her toes and persuaded her into the kiss this time, starting soft and gentle and working into hard and demanding. When they were both breathless, he lifted his head and looked down into her dazed face. He smiled. "Tell me you're staying home tonight."

"I—"

"Better yet, tell me you're staying with *me* tonight."

"Logan." She frowned at him. "Remember, your mother—"

He cut her off with another long, drugging kiss. "We'll tell her we need privacy."

"No!"

His smile turned wicked. "Okay, we'll tell *Gabby* we need privacy."

"Oh." Elena's shoulders sagged. "Gabby. For a minute you made me forget why I came home."

"There's something wrong with Gabby?"

"No, no, no." Elena slid out of his arms. "It's just that I need to talk to her."

Logan didn't like the shadow of worry darkening her eyes. "Can I help?"

She shook her head. "No, it's fine." With a distracted air, she looked around and spotted the purse and bag she'd dropped when he grabbed her. "I have to get this over with, though."

Logan's hands fisted. "It would be nice to know what 'this' is."

"What?" She blinked at him, then shook her head. "It's not your problem," she said, then turned away from him.

His temper rocketing, Logan stared at her retreating back. "Elena!"

She glanced over her shoulder. "Hmm?"

He forced himself to sound civil. "Will I see you later?"

Her answer was non-committal, her feet were speedy going up the stairs. Steaming, Logan stalked back into the bathroom, gripped the sledgehammer, then pounded it against the tiled shower. Oh, she was so damn good, he thought, trying to destroy his frustration with another swing. So damn good at creating those physical and emotional distances that he was beginning to believe she'd never let him near.

Elena's hand trembled as she tried to fit the key into the lock of the apartment door. Weariness, she thought. Day job, part-time job, college course, the prom coming up in a little more than a week, they all added up to not enough sleep and probably not enough to eat, either.

A little dinner, a little down time, she'd be good as new. Her shoulders slumped, knowing that neither rest or refueling would ease the weight of her conscience.

Loud thumps—Logan pounding at something in the bathroom downstairs—made her wince. No doubt about it, he was mad, and no way around it, she had to take the blame.

She'd agreed to be his lover and then done everything she could to avoid him as often as she could. But it wasn't because she didn't *want* to be with him. That was the whole problem.

It was too good with him. Too pleasureful, too addictive.

Too easy to want to trust. Too easy to depend on. Too, too, too.

Elena sucked in a breath and firmed her grip on the key. She'd have to elude him as much as possible for just a few more days to keep all those "toos" under control. In a short time her house would be repaired. Then she'd be back on her familiar block and back in her familiar surroundings. Once she and Logan didn't share the same roof, his interest in her would wane, and she would bury her interest in him under all that it took to get Gabby ready for college.

Gabby... Her conscience twinged again, but she straightened her shoulders, focused on the lock, had success inserting the key. Another violent thump sounded from downstairs and Elena gritted her teeth as she swung open the door. It was time to see who else she could tick off today.

Her sister was sitting at the card table, surrounded by books, her binder open. She looked up as Elena shut the door behind her. "Hello," she said politely.

Elena gritted her teeth again. Gabby had been different, though oh-so-polite since the day Logan had witnessed their exchange of words over her art and Tyler. It was only normal, Elena tried telling herself. Gabby was beginning to assert her independence in these last few months before going off to Berkeley.

But a dry ache burned at the back of Elena's eyes. It was going to be strange, lonely and strange, when her little sister left. Gabby had been the focus of all her energy and emotion for so long. Realization of a dream or not, the absence of Gabby would leave a hole that even the satisfaction of her enrollment in pre-med at Berkeley wouldn't fill.

But looking at her sister, Elena wondered if Gabby would feel anything close to the same. Because it was obvious that irritation at Elena, not independence from her, was the primary emotion driving Gabby now.

Still, Elena managed a smile. "Well, hello to you too," she replied. "I haven't seen much of you the past couple of days."

Gabby went back to her books. "Mmm."

"I hope you don't think I've been neglecting you."

"I know you're busy at work."

"Right." Guilt stabbed Elena again. She should have resolved the argument with Gabby immediately, instead of letting it fester. "I—"

"The boutique called. My prom dress came in. May I use the car later to go get it?"

Elena nodded. "Sure." The clerk at the specialty shop where Gabby had found *the* perfect dress had found it in *the* perfect size at another store in the chain. She cleared her throat. "About the prom..."

Gabby must have heard the bad news in her voice. She looked up, her gaze narrowing. "What?"

Elena cleared her throat again. "I'mchaperoning." The two words rushed out as one.

Gabby's jaw dropped. *"What?"*

Elena flushed, feeling guilty all over again. "We're short of chaperons and..." and Elena's inattention at one of the meetings had somehow translated into her volunteering "...and we're still short. I know you asked me not to, but I can't get out of it."

Gabby's face turned red. "You promised. I only asked of you *one* thing when you volunteered for the senior prom committee, and you *promised.*"

"I know, I know. But we also promised the school administration there would be enough parents on hand that night." Elena smiled, trying to lighten the situation. "Apparently almost every senior in school made their mom and dad take a blood oath not to attend."

"But you won't live up to *your* promise."

"Come on, Gabriellita, how bad could it be?" Elena understood her sister's worry that she might wet-blanket her fun, but really, how wild was Gabby likely to get? She shrugged away the nagging worry that thought brought to mind. "Most people would choose a sister as chaperon over a parent any day."

"Most people don't have *you* for a sister," Gabby retorted.

Elena refused to let her feelings be hurt. Gabby was

a teenager, after all, and up until recently their relationship had been amazingly conflict-free. "I'm sorry, Gab, I really am. I'll stay out of your hair that night. I will."

Gabby jumped to her feet and began slamming her open books shut. "Oh yeah, right."

Stunned by the bitterness in Gabby's sarcastic agreement, Elena stared at her. Then she swallowed. "Is there…is there something wrong? This sounds like more than disappointment about the prom."

With jerky movements, Gabby shoved books and papers into her backpack. "Since when have you become Sister Sensitive? Since when have you cared anything about what I feel?"

Elena's heart flinched at the blow. This was her family talking, her only family, the one who would achieve for her, for their mother, for Nana. "Gabby…" Elena's voice was so hoarse she had to start over. "Gabby, I don't understand what's going on with you. Have you and Tyler had a fight?"

Gabby slung her backpack over her shoulder. "No! The best part of my life is Tyler. He's the only one who understands me and cares about what I want."

The only one who cares about what she wants? "And…and what exactly is that?" Even as Elena told herself Gabby's outburst was merely senior-itis or maybe pre-college jitters, she wrapped her arms around her waist, hugging herself for comfort. "What is it you want, Gabby?"

Her sister's mouth drew to a firm, stubborn line. "I

want to go to Acton, not Berkeley. I want to study art, not medicine.''

If Gabby had grown another head, Elena couldn't be more shocked. ''No,'' she said automatically. ''Berkeley, pre-med, then med school, those are your dreams.''

''They're *your* dreams *for* me.''

''You never said—''

''I've said it dozens of times in dozens of different ways. But you haven't listened.''

''No.'' Elena shook her head. ''You never said.''

Gabby drew herself up to her full five feet two inches. ''Well then, I'm saying it now. As a matter of fact, I contacted Acton this week and accepted their offer.''

There was an odd roaring in Elena's ears. Like a vacuum, she thought. It was the sound of emptiness. Empty dreams. Then she shook her head again, trying to shake the strange noise away.

''This is about Tyler,'' she heard herself saying. ''That's what this is. Tyler's going to Acton, he wants you there, and now you've let him get to you.'' Suddenly she was in front of her sister and she grabbed Gabby's shoulder to give it a little shake. ''Listen to me. You can't do this. You can't depend on him when the only thing you can count on is that he'll break your heart.''

As Logan lifted the sledgehammer again, he caught sight of a reflection in the mirror on the opposite wall and started in surprise. Who the hell was that? A dust-covered, rock-jawed, hungry-eyed stranger stared back.

Elena had transformed him, turned him into someone he didn't know, someone who felt barely in control of himself.

Disgusted, he threw the sledgehammer down. Leaving the mess just as it was, he strode upstairs, not sparing a glance toward Elena and Gabby's door. Instead, he went straight for his own apartment, then straight to his bathroom. After a cold shower that improved his looks but not his hot mood, he stalked to the kitchen.

His mother was in there, but she said nothing as he jerked open the refrigerator and then downed half a beer in one long swallow. He held the sweating bottle against his forehead, then brought it back to his mouth to drain it dry.

The empty bottle clacked loudly against the countertop before he dove back into the refrigerator for another. His mother spoke while he was wrestling it out of the depths of the cardboard twelve-pack.

"Is something wrong, Logan?" she asked.

He backed out with his beer and shook his head. "Nothing that a half-dozen of these won't fix."

She cocked an eyebrow at him. "Of course, your father thinks the world's a much more civilized place after his seven o'clock martini, but this doesn't seem like you, Logan."

He took a swallow, then saluted his mother with the bottle. "A point to Mrs. Chase. You've just hit the nail on the head. I'm not myself and I very much resent it.''

His mother nodded. ''Ah. Elena, I presume.''

He didn't bother to ask how she'd figured it out. ''That woman is too much trouble.''

''You've always liked your life carefree.''

''Exactly.''

''It can't be easy to have to think about what someone else needs and wants.''

Logan narrowed his eyes. ''Ha ha ha, Mom. But you're off target this time. The problem is, Elena doesn't want or need anything from me.''

''You're sure.''

He ignored her skeptical tone. ''I'm sure. And I'm over it, too. That woman hasn't left my head for eleven years, but enough's enough.'' With a violent gesture, he banged the nearly full beer down on the counter.

''Where are you going?'' his mother asked mildly.

He hadn't even realized he was at the kitchen doorway. ''To...to tell her. I'm not a hotheaded, passionate man and I refuse to let her make me feel like one!''

He wanted his uncomplicated, rational world back. He wanted his uncomplicated, rational *self* back. He slammed out of his apartment and was halfway to Elena's when the sound of an angry female voice floating through the hall pierced his inflamed mood. Pausing, he...

Well, hell, he couldn't help but eavesdrop.

The door to the other apartment was ajar and small

fingers were gripping the edge of it as if the owner of the hand was just pausing to get in a few last words. "I'm going to make my own decisions from now on, Elena, decisions that work for me. I won't let you use my life to prove to people how untouchable, how unbeatable the O'Briens are. My becoming a doctor was your slap in the face to anyone who ever hurt you—most importantly a slap in the face to our father for leaving us. But I won't let you use me like that anymore."

With that, Gabby whirled out the door, then whirled back. "I'm spending the night at Mandy's." Then she slammed the door and without a glance toward Logan, headed down the stairs, her purse and backpack bumping against each tread behind her.

Logan blew out a long breath. As lousy as his mood was, only the lowest of the low would dump on Elena now. Not that she'd probably give a rat's behind that he was breaking things off between them—more likely she'd sigh in relief—but he imagined she was busy hunkering down right now, clutching to herself whatever she was feeling after her latest argument with Gabby.

As he turned to go back to his apartment though, he heard the sound of her door opening again. Surprised, he turned back.

She was staring at him, her face expressionless, but a little pale.

"If you're thinking about going after Gabby," he said, "she's already left."

Elena shook her head.

He took a step toward her, then stopped himself. She wouldn't welcome his sympathy and he didn't want how she made him feel anymore. He didn't want the intensity, the confusion, the only-temporary satisfaction that slaking his lust with her brought.

"Logan," she said. It was more of a croak, really, and her eyes were focused on his face. "Logan, I...I was coming to find you."

He frowned. "Why?"

She hesitated. Then her face crumpled and she ran toward him.

He caught her in his arms. Her tears were already hot on his neck as he carried her back into her apartment. "Shh," he said against her hair. He shut the door with his foot, then slid down against it so she was safe in the cradle of his lap and arms. "Shh. Shh."

Hell, he might as well have tried to shush the tide. Shuddering in his arms, she cried and cried. He patted her back, smoothed her hair, thought about calling his mother, but then couldn't imagine himself relinquishing his hold of her.

She wept with the same fervency with which she'd crushed his corsage beneath her toe all those years ago. It was as if she'd stored up years' worth of emotions and now she had to release them. She was still sobbing, her eyes overflowing when she looked up at him and tried to talk. "Gabby—you—" Her breath caught, rough and thick in her throat.

He pushed her hair away from her hot forehead. "Tell me later," he said softly, then started to move her so he could find them both a more comfortable place to sit.

Her arms clutched at him. "No."

"Okay, okay." He regathered her against him and let her weep some more, until finally she subsided into shuddering breaths punctuated here and there by a hiccup.

He continued to hold her though, until he felt her stir. His arms loosened and she restlessly wiggled her behind against him. Familiar—if untimely—lust caused blood to rush toward his lap. He eased her to the floor beside him to save them both embarrassment.

She didn't protest, just instantly drew her knees up to her chest and buried her face against them, wrapping her arms around her legs. It was a self-contained, self-comforting, Elena-back-to-Elena pose.

Resigned, Logan let out the air he didn't realize he'd been holding. Despite her brief storm of emotion, he doubted anything had really changed. Elena wouldn't share herself with him and he in turn would only grow more frustrated with her.

Better to get out now, he told himself again, when there was little damage done.

"Will you be fine now?" he asked. Of course she would be. She was always fine. Or she always would say so, anyway.

She lifted her head and looked at him. "No," she said, then wiped her nose with the back of her hand like a child. "No, I'm not fine." A fresh wave of tears overflowed her eyes to run down her face.

"Elena." Logan's heart stilled in his chest. "Elena, what is it?"

"Y-you." Her voice caught in another hard sob. "I n-need y-you."

He stared at her, his heart restarting, then starting to race. Her eyelashes were spiked, her nose was red, her cheeks and forehead were splotchy from crying. Just as his accelerating heart seemed to crest a hill and take a roller-coaster dive, he felt the strangest urge to laugh. For all her incredible beauty, Elena wasn't a pretty crier.

It made her all at once more real, more dear…

More his.

He buried that thought as she mutely held out her arms toward him. His heart zipped around a curve then climbed as he once more lifted her onto his lap.

"You've been working too hard," he murmured to her. "You need to sleep more, eat more often." He suddenly remembered the day when she'd arrived at the Victorian dizzy with exhaustion. A rush of tenderness swept through him and he was excruciatingly aware of how small she was, of how much energy and strength usually poured out of such a delicate body.

Elena said something against his shirt.

He cuddled her close. "What, honey? I didn't hear."

"Gabby's m-mad."

"I know." He rested his cheek on top of Elena's head. "A sister spat. I know one when I see one.

Brothers bicker, sisters spat. Nothing to worry about.''

She was shaking her head. Then she drew away from his chest to look at him. Using both hands, she swiped at her wet face. "I d-don't have a heart." Her voice still broke with emotion. "She s-said I don't have a heart."

"Oh, Elena." The hurt on her face slayed him, it did, because he'd been thinking nearly the very same thing when he stomped up the stairs not long ago.

"Am I really so cold?"

"No." She was careful, he thought. Gabby had seen that too. Untouchable. Unbeatable. That's what Elena wanted everyone to *think.* "No, you're not cold at all."

Elena closed her eyes. "I've messed things up with Gabby. I've messed things up with you." Those wet, heavy-looking lashes lifted and her lower lip trembled. "I'm sorry. I'm so sorry."

Oh, hell. She *was* trouble. But the stranger she turned him into couldn't let that trouble go.

Chapter Twelve

Elena couldn't remember the last time she'd let herself cry. It was a sure thing that she'd never before let herself cry in a man's arms.

That thought had her struggling finally to break free of Logan's lap, but his arms only tightened around her. She settled back against his chest for a moment, forced to close her eyes against the sweetness of that close embrace.

She must be out of tears, right? But she squeezed her eyes tight anyway, unwilling to take the chance that he would guess she could be so silly, so *weak*, as to cry over him.

As it was, he had to find her and all this weepiness, this neediness, foolish.

She'd confessed that Gabby called her cold-hearted.

She'd apologized to Logan for messing things up between them.

Oh, God. He must be embarrassed for her. She was embarrassed for *herself*.

Now desperate to regain her dignity, she pushed away from his chest and tried drying her face with her palms. "I'm fine now," she said. "You can let me go."

"You're fine now," Logan repeated slowly, something unfamiliar coming to life in his eyes. "I can let you go."

A little spooked, she made to move completely off him, but was once again caught, his hands gripping her arms. "Yeah, fine." She swallowed, even trying on what felt like a weak smile. "Sorry that I did the tear thing all over you, but I'm really okay."

His nostrils flared and his palms seemed to burn against the flesh of her arms.

Spooked again, she looked away. She had to clear her mind, think of Gabby, realize that Logan's embrace, Logan's heat wasn't necessary to her. "Just tired," she mumbled again, more to herself than him. "Tired but fi—"

"Shut up," Logan said. "For once just shut up." Then he yanked her forward to take her mouth.

Elena's brains scrambled. The kiss was devastating. No persuasive softness, no seductive brush of lip on lip, just his mouth pushing hers open, seeking her tongue, her taste. Her nipples tightened in a rush. A shudder raced down her back, goose bumps ran the same path. Oh, she needed this too.

She leaned into the kiss, there was no helping herself, taking his desire as she'd taken his comfort, with her heart open.

But then she found herself jerking back, some self-protective instinct still breathing inside her. *I can't.* Her feet scuffed against the polished hardwood floor, trying to find purchase. *I can't do this now.*

Not when her emotions were riding so close to the surface. Not when her heart was so willing to let him in.

She pushed against his chest, half rose. "I've got to get up."

With one quick movement, he tumbled her back into his arms. "No. I won't let you back away from me again."

There was something implacable beneath the hoarse softness of Logan's voice. Her gaze shot to his and she saw it there, too, a sharp intent under all the molten gold.

"Don't you see I need you too, Elena?" His fingers were gripping her arms at the elbow, but he gently stroked the inner skin with his thumbs. "I've missed you."

"But—"

"Let me." His eyes were burning hot, his gaze like fire on her mouth. "I have to have you. I have to have you *now*."

Elena hesitated, she needed him, wanted him so much too. But it was probably too much! Too—

The thought went unfinished as he rolled and put her beneath him. Her skirt was shoved up her thighs as he came between her legs, his body heavy, heated. Doubt was drowned in desire.

He rocked against her, making more room for himself, making her dizzy with wanting him with only that small movement. His hands brushed her hair from her face. The gesture was a tender one, but Elena could feel the tension in his fingers. Need was driving him, she knew it, and an answering pulse started throbbing between her thighs, low and deep.

He lowered his head and kissed her again. Elena's eyes drifted shut. The kiss was softer this time, leashed ruthlessly back, but her body was compelled to lift to his nonetheless, her pelvis tilting to find its match. The deep pulse between her legs pounded. Gentle, hard, soft, demanding, no matter how he asked, her body was insisting she comply.

Stop. She thought the word, it was a command to herself after all. There might be no way to prevent herself from acting on the urge to do this with him, but she could stop herself from letting her passion rage. That would be her undoing.

That would be his way into her soul.

She forced her eyes open as he lifted his mouth. His face was bare of any expression but need, the angles of his jaw and cheekbones sharper, almost lethal-looking. Elena's heart jumped, then raced as he slid down her body to explore her neck with his mouth.

There was a stubble of golden beard on his cheeks and chin and he rubbed them against her, following their path with his tongue. Heat shot through her body, and Elena forced a half-choked breath into her lungs, trying to hold on to her control.

She closed her eyes again and tried to separate herself from the dangerous craving by imagining she was watching the two of them from a distance. The rangy, golden-haired man, his body over the woman's. She was panting a little, sure, but it was all right, because the man's mouth was drifting lower, toward the V of the woman's collar. Who wouldn't pant?

His tongue painted something wicked and wonderful against the pulse at her throat. Elena jolted, her eyes flying open. Logan's head lifted and she saw that his pupils were large black pools. His mouth was wet and his breath was loud in her ears.

He caught her gaze. Held it. Elena tried to shut her eyes against him, she tried to find that protective distance again, but then his fingers curled into the edges of her blouse.

"You do this to me," he said, his voice hard and guttural. "Only you."

He tore the material apart. Buttons pinged, skittered, hitting the floor then dancing away. His fingers moved, fast and sure, to the clasp of her bra.

No hesitation, no trembling, nothing but needing. Having.

He bared her to him and sank lower to take her breast.

Elena's body bowed.

Distance, separation, none of it was possible. Not when his hands were soft on her, caressing, stoking fires, then hard, no finesse at all as he tossed away the rest of her clothes.

It was raging now. Passion breaking free of the cage where she'd locked it so long ago. It didn't matter anymore what might break free with it. She couldn't think about that—couldn't think at all.

Somehow, Logan's clothes were gone too. She knew she'd undressed him, she could even see a thin welt along his chest where her fingernail had caught him in her impetuous, impatient need. Shoving him to his back, she put her mouth there, licking the little wound until her tongue encountered the bump of his nipple.

She heard him groan, felt his body flinch. Without even thinking, she fastened her mouth over it and sucked.

Under her hand, his heartbeat thundered. It tripped up her own heart, then hers caught his rhythm and raced along with it.

Her mouth following her hand, Elena smoothed her fingers across his chest, then down. Her pinky brushed something hard, smooth, so hot that she jerked. But then *it* jerked, and she soothed it with her palm.

She stroked him, marveling at the smooth skin, the heat. Her skin felt hot too, maybe hotter than his, she thought. Leaning over him, her breast brushed his belly, her tongue slid down his hard column of flesh.

In the blink of an eye, her shoulders thumped against the floor. It didn't hurt, there was no pain in

Logan's body over hers again, sliding down hers again, lifting her knees then opening her to his mouth.

At the very first touch, pleasure burst. Elena choked on a scream, and then lost her voice altogether when he ignored the telltale shudders of her body and touched her again, tasted her again, over and over. Though she was still quivering from the first release, he held her hips and demanded she rise.

His fingers were hard on her thighs, his mouth insistent. This wasn't the good-natured, easygoing Logan. This wasn't the cool charmer who could make her feel sixteen by raising one amused eyebrow.

This was a man, demanding, insisting, stopping at less than nothing to expose a woman's every need, every secret, every secret desire.

Pleasure at that tightest of coils once again, her hips lifted. His mouth slowed.

She tried digging her fingers into the cool wood floor. She tried breathing through her desperate anticipation.

"No one can make you feel this way," Logan said, his voice coming from a long distance. "No one but me."

Of course, of course! she screamed in her mind. No one had ever, ever made her feel this way.

"Say it," he demanded, his voice low and possessive. "Say it."

Her mind scrambled, trying to understand what he wanted. *Don't admit it,* some worried voice said inside her. *He wants everything.*

But if he took that, if he took everything, then she'd have nothing left.

Elena's gaze flew to him. He was sitting up now, his eyes trained on her face. Almost casually, he reached down to where she was left throbbing and unsatisfied and caressed her with one finger.

Elena squirmed.

"Say it."

She swallowed, trying to think.

He caressed her again.

She shivered, broke. "You," she said. "No one but you."

In one smooth move, he dropped down and she felt the soft, wet touch of his tongue. She shivered hard, once, shattered.

And then he drew up and drove his body inside hers, pushing through the waves of her release so that he *was* the release, he owned it, he owned *her*.

She should deny it, thrust him away, but instead she clutched at his shoulders, then slid her hands toward his hips as he buried his face against her neck. His body surged powerfully into hers.

"Elena," he said hoarsely. "So good. So right."

So right. Another wave hit her, unexpected and hard. Her body gripped his to ride it out and he stiffened, surged once more, deep, deep.

And became hers.

For the second time in her life, for the second time that day, she cried in Logan's arms.

She hid her tears against his shoulder, praying he would never know how weak he made her.

* * *

She was only one of fifty or so people in the high-school auditorium, all of them readying it for the up-coming senior prom. But Logan thought he could poll ten times that number of men and they would unan-imously agree that the most eye-catching, the sexiest female in the place was Elena O'Brien.

She was *his* sexy female, and if he had his way, he was going to be her date to the dance Saturday night.

Smiling smugly to himself, Logan strolled toward the ladder she was perched on. Large cardboard boxes surrounded it, as well as a scattering of tools, and Elena's totebag and purse. She was completely obliv-ious to his approach as she studied a sheet of paper in one hand. In the other, she held a dinner-plate-size flower that appeared to be created from stiff, brightly colored fabric.

Coming up behind her, he found that by lifting his gaze he made it level with her glorious behind, briefly covered by a short denim skirt. Curling his fingers around a leg of the ladder, he smiled again, appreci-ating the view.

"Ricky Dodd, are you trying to look up my skirt again?" Elena suddenly hissed, without glancing away from the paper. "Because if you are I'm telling your mother."

Look up her skirt again? Lifting an eyebrow, he ran a possessive finger from her bare ankle up the back of her thigh to the hem of the skirt, satisfied by her little yelp and the rush of goose bumps he left in his path. "Isn't one man enough for you?" he teased.

Her foot jerked back and he captured it just before it caught him in the gut. "Careful, careful, can't have you falling off the ladder."

She was glaring at him over her shoulder. "If I did, I'd fall right on top of you."

He grinned. "Promises, promises." At the exasperated purse of her delicious lips, he laughed and tugged lightly on the leg he held. "C'mere."

"Why?" Her eyes narrowed.

"So suspicious." He tugged again. "I want to kiss you."

"No." She shook her head. "Not a good idea. I have a lot of work to do here and kissing you distracts me."

Pleased, he smiled again. Then instead of bothering with more cajoling, he merely climbed up behind her. Standing on the rung below hers, their heads level, he turned her face toward him.

She made another murmuring protest, but he was getting better at ignoring her talk—especially when he was intent on her taste. Her mouth pucker-kissed his for a second, but then her lips softened. He teased their seam with the tip of his tongue until he felt her whole body sag and her mouth open.

She was hot and wet inside and...

Logan wrenched his mouth away and leaped off the ladder, then grabbed it to make sure his sudden movement didn't tip Elena over. "You're dangerous," he muttered.

Her cheeks were bright pink and her eyes sparked at him. "It was *your* idea."

"Yeah, yeah, yeah." But he had to grin, because she didn't look as much mad as she looked... interested. He tickled the back of her knee. "When will you be done here?"

She slapped at his hand with the paper she held. "Never, if you keep doing things like that."

He took an instant step back. "Hands off, then. I want to see you tonight." Suddenly it seemed a much better idea to be alone when he brought up the prom. If any persuasion was necessary, he wanted to be able to use whatever measures came to mind.

Her gaze slid back to her paper, and he could see it specified the decorations for this part of the auditorium. "You're seeing me now," she said. "It's night."

"I want to see you naked."

"Shh!" Her head jerked up and she whipped it around, making sure no one had overheard his remark. Apparently assured that they were reasonably private, she frowned at him. "You saw me naked last night."

And it had been as wild as the night she'd cried in his arms and then tried to pull away from him. Just like that time, last night the heat, the beast inside him had clawed its way out and he'd unleashed everything he had on Elena. Controlling himself around her was more and more of an effort, and he was less and less successful at it.

He gently stroked her leg again. "Are you all right?"

Throwing him a frustrated look, she backed down

the ladder. "Why do you keep asking me that?" She tossed the flower she held into one of the nearby boxes and walked over to another, pulling out something that looked like a banana leaf. "I'm not some hothouse rose."

No, Logan thought. She was something much more exotic and unique. He caught a breath of her delicious scent and remembered it on him, on his hands, his clothes, after their lovemaking the night before.

He walked over to her. "I don't like thinking I might have bruised you." His hand stroked the back of her hair.

She leaned a little into his touch. "I believe you later verified for yourself that I was perfectly fine."

Inch by inch. But she hadn't been completely unmarked. She'd had beard burn on her neck and her belly. A fingertip-size bruise on the underside of one breast. He'd still be apologizing for that and more, except Elena had stifled his first round with a kiss that nearly blew off the top of his head.

She liked it, she'd said. She liked knowing that he wasn't always so cool.

Oh, little, little did she know how un-cool she made him with just a smile, a touch, one look at her incredible face. It was damn unsettling and it was also something he'd vowed to get a better handle on.

The beep of her watch alarm sounded and she hurried away from him to rummage through her tote bag. Logan watched her extract the shoebox and the journal that was part of her class project.

"That's *still* not over with?"

She shook her head. "Couple more days. I'm hoping for an A. I heard that I'm one of the few who hasn't damaged, abandoned or brought her eggs back to the instructor for adoption."

Until this moment, he'd forgotten that her alarm had gone off that first wild night, too. But now he remembered that she'd gotten up to "feed" the twins, while he'd merely grunted then rolled into the warm space on the futon where her body had been, leaving barely a blip in his sleep pattern.

It was stupid to feel a guilty jab of conscience, they certainly weren't *his* kids, but for a second he knew what it felt like to be the kind of man who left all the dirty diapers and night feedings to his wife.

He cleared his throat and looked away, trying to think of something other than wives, husbands and Elena-as-mother. A familiar dark head moving in the distance caught his attention.

"How are things with Gabby?" he asked. Elena had told him they'd agreed to a temporary truce the day after their latest argument.

"The same. We've agreed to cool off for a few days and not talk about the future until after the prom's over."

"Mmm." Now his focus was captured by another movement, closer by. A young high-school stud, his T-shirt sleeves rolled up to display bulging biceps, paraded in front of Elena, boxes in his arms.

He was walking by so slowly and his gaze was so stuck on Elena that Logan would have plenty of time to stride over and yank on the tongue that was hang-

ing out of the kid's mouth. "Hey, Elena," the kid
called out with a cocky grin. "Can I give you a hand
or two?"

Elena looked up. "Thanks very much, Ian, but you
can keep your hands to yourself." She softened the
blow with a smile, though, and Logan saw her eyes
warm. "You been working out or something?"

"Yeah." The kid's grin turned from cocky to delighted. "Yeah."

Elena grinned back. "Lookin' good, Ian. Lookin'
real good."

His chest popping farther forward, the boy swag-
gered off.

Floored, Logan gazed on the woman who had once
again managed to surprise him. She noticed his stare
and frowned. "What? What are you looking at me
like that for?"

"You were…you were actually nice to that kid."

She scowled, the same scowl that he'd been on the
receiving end of for months. The same scowl that
he'd always thought every male received from her.
"I can be nice."

"I think you might have been—" he coughed, trying to get the word out "—flirting with him."

"I was not *flirting* with him." She rolled her eyes.
"He's a friend of Gabby's for goodness sake. I've
known him since he liked to play with G.I. Joe."

"I don't think it's G.I. Joe he wants to play with
now."

She frowned and rolled her eyes again. "His girlfriend just broke up with him, okay? He's been feel-

ing a little blue about going to the dance Saturday night stag.''

"Stag? Boys go the prom stag? It's not couples only?''

Elena shook her head. "Times have changed, Logan. Both boys and girls go to the prom alone or in a big group. There'll be plenty of dateless kids there."

"Dateless boys.''

She shrugged.

He could see her on Saturday night now, taking on the task of ego-boosting every young stud by smiling at them, or flirting with them, or worse yet, *dancing* with them, while he sat home alone. Hell yes, he was going to be her date.

A sudden idea occurred to him. With all this new-found sympathy of hers, maybe he could get *her* to ask *him*. It was a satisfying thought. "My mother said she's lending you a dress for the dance."

She half-knelt to tuck the twins and journal away. "Yes, and it's very nice of her. She overheard me talking to Gabby about needing something to wear when I was going down the stairs yesterday. She volunteered a gown of hers that she thinks might do."

"I'd sure like to see it." Hint, hint.

"Have her show it to you," Elena said, standing. Then she paused, looking at him closely. "What's this all about?"

Smart girl. "I don't know what you mean." He slid his hands in his pockets, looking innocent, and, he hoped, irresistible. Because he'd decided that re-playing the night of the prom, replaying it without hitches, without heartache, would erase that first time from her mind. With the slate clean, she could begin to trust him, truly trust him.

When she remained silent, he thought he'd give her a little nudge. "It's just that, well, I don't have a thing to do on Saturday night."

She retreated a step. "What?"

Hell, did he have to spell it out? "My mother is still not speaking to my father and she's still living with me. If I stay home alone on Saturday night, she'll cook. Last time it was Sloppy Joe Surprise with something called Cottage Cheese Cauliflower Bake as a side dish. Then there's bridge lessons. Have I mentioned I hate bridge?"

Her hand crept up toward her heart. "This isn't a good idea."

He tamped down a flare of irritation. "Why not?"

"I don't know." She shook her head, looking more wary than such a simple thing warranted.

"Elena—" He broke off as a pair of high-school boys ambled near, their overabundant and underused hormones visible in their overeager and undersubtle expressions. They were looking at Elena as if she was the living embodiment of every fantasy that kept them awake nights.

And she was, damn it. But they were *his* fantasies and she was *his* Elena. He glowered at them.

They didn't appear to know he was alive. "Hi, Elena," one boy said, slicking his surfer-blond hair back with his palm. "Heard you're coming to the prom."

"That's right, Jay. You have a big night planned?"

He shrugged, grinned. "Maybe now I do."

Elena laughed. "I'll let you bring me a glass of punch."

There was a twinkle in the boy's blue eyes that was probably as cute as all get out to Elena, but only served to piss Logan off.

His mood only got worse when the other kid spoke up. "Wanna dance?" he abruptly said, his face immediately flushing.

Elena smiled. "I suppose you don't mean right now, do you, Carl?"

"No, no." The kid's face went even redder. "I mean Saturday night. Wanna dance Saturday night?"

"That sounds wonderful," Elena said, in a voice so soft and sweet that it gave Logan a jolt. "I'll look forward to it."

With that success, the boys hurried off, the surfer clapping Carl on the back in hearty congratulations.

Logan watched them, his mood getting darker by the moment. "Maybe you'll be too busy for me Saturday night," he heard himself say. "Maybe you already have a date with Dudley Studly there, or some other kid who needs a dance lesson or a shoulder to cry on."

Elena blinked, then her lips twitched. "You're jealous."

He tried shrugging the stupid feeling away, but it clung to his back like a monkey. "That's not it." It wasn't jealousy. No matter what he'd just said, he didn't resent her dancing or talking with those high-school boys. What was driving him now was something else, some edge-of-desperation feeling she invariably brought out in him.

She crossed her arms over her chest, looking just the tiniest bit too happy. "That's why you want to go to the prom with me. You're jealous."

Fine, Logan thought with disgust. Let her think it. It only made him more irritated, but he'd let her think whatever was necessary in order to be her date. The prom was a bridge they needed to cross. It would take her to trust. It would take him to…peace. Peace and control.

Once Elena was no longer fighting him so hard he was sure he'd return to his old, assured and in-control self. He was tired of feeling like a stranger in his own skin. "You're going with me to the prom," he ground out, then walked off, giving her no other chance to argue or refuse.

Chapter Thirteen

The decorating committee knocked off around 10:00 p.m. and Elena drove Gabby home, Logan following in his own car. After surprising her by showing up in the auditorium and then surprising her again by insisting on being her prom date, he'd ended up helping a group of volunteers at the other end of the building.

There were only two days left to transform the functional but ugly auditorium interior into a lush Garden of Eden. One crew worked a few hours during the day, while another, larger crew was working the evening shift. Elena still worried it would not be completed on time.

She glanced over at Gabby, her sister's profile dark against the glow from the dashboard lights. "What do you think, Gab? Are we going to make it by seven Saturday night?''

''No problem.'' Gabby flapped a hand in dismissal. ''But I'll get everybody from my fourth-period art class to work during lunch tomorrow, if that will make you feel any better.''

Since Gabby's fourth-period art class had designed the elaborate scenery, it did make Elena feel somewhat better. She continued to chew on her bottom lip, though. ''Maybe Logan will help out tomorrow night too.''

''If you ask, he will. He's got a stake in it now, right? He said he's going to be your date.''

Elena glanced over again, wondering whether to avoid or confront the touchy subject. ''Is that a problem?'' she asked hesitantly. ''I know you don't want me there. If Logan makes it worse I can tell him to forget it.'' Relief rippled through her. It would be the perfect excuse to renege on a yes she technically hadn't given to him anyway.

''It's fine with me.''

Elena sighed, but didn't pursue the subject. She was already on eggshells around her sister, and it was better not to do or say anything that might upset the uneasy harmony between them.

Except that when they walked into the Victorian to find their mail waiting on the small table beside the door, Elena couldn't control her expressions—verbal and facial—of dismay as she stared down at the thick envelope from the Acton School addressed to Gabby.

"You weren't joking?" she said, staring at her sister. "You actually contacted Acton and accepted?"

Gabby snatched the envelope from her hand. "Of course I wasn't joking."

Elena shook her head, a sick feeling rising and falling like waves in her stomach. "Gabby—"

"We had a truce," her sister said, her voice tight. "No talk about this until after Saturday night."

Elena heard Logan come through the front door behind her, but she ignored him. "I don't care about any truce now. I—"

"Don't," Logan said in her ear, his breath soft and warm against it. "Not now."

Elena spun toward him, then spun back as she heard footsteps dashing up the stairs. "Gabby…" The door to their apartment slammed behind her sister.

Her gaze cut toward Logan. "Thanks a lot."

"You're welcome."

She made a face at him. "I have an auditorium that may never look like Paradise, a headache the size of the Pacific, and a little sister who would like my head on a platter. This is not the time for funny."

He put his hands on her shoulders and massaged the muscles there. "Give me the chance to make you feel better then."

Elena frowned, thinking again of his insistence on attending the prom with her. Her misgivings weren't easy to verbalize, but they were just added weight to her shoulders. "You *should* make me feel better," she grumbled.

His hands still working their magic, he directed her

into the small parlor. The shabby recliners and the big-screen TV remained the only furnishings, but he'd removed all the old wallpaper and stripped the paint off the wainscoting and window trim to reveal intricate woodwork that gleamed in the soft glow of a small lamp. "It's beautiful, Logan," she said, awed by the change. "I can't believe how much work you've accomplished."

He took her purse and her tote bag from her and set them beside one of the recliners. Then he dropped into the big chair and drew her down on his lap so he could return to kneading her tight muscles. "When it's something you enjoy doing, it doesn't seem like work. On the other hand, I used to dread mornings because mornings meant going to Chase Electronics."

She adjusted her position, sitting across his lap so she could look at him. "Really? You actually dreaded it?"

He nodded. "Yeah. What's worse, my father and Griffin love the business so much that it only added to my misery. I felt guilty for how much I hated it."

Elena frowned, then leaned forward to lightly kiss his mouth. "Then I'm even more glad for you that you're now doing what *you* want."

His gaze didn't leave hers. "Are you, Elena? Are you really glad?"

She nodded. "Of course."

"Then maybe you should think about being glad for Gabby too."

Elena's spine stiffened. "I thought you were going

to make me feel better. Talking about Gabby right now isn't going to do that."

"I'll talk about me, then."

Elena squirmed. "Come on—"

"I was miserable for more years than I care to count because I went along with what my family expected of me. Not just in the business, but in the women I dated. Damn it, Elena, don't do that to Gabby. Don't design her life for her and expect her to follow it to the letter."

She jumped to her feet. "I'm not *designing* her life. I'm helping to direct her talents." Hearing herself, she shook her head. "No, no, that sounds as if she doesn't know her own mind."

Logan's eyebrows lifted. "So you concede that she has her own mind? That she knows exactly what she wants?"

"Of course she does!" Elena hissed at him. "She's got the brains and the tenacity to be a doctor."

"But does she have the will?"

"She has the will to be anything," Elena shot at him. "Anything."

"Maybe her will—and more importantly her heart—tells her she should be an artist."

Elena found herself restless and edgy, so she started pacing the small room, as if she could walk off the feelings. "She wants to be an artist because she's infatuated with Tyler and *he* wants to be an artist. As soon as her interest in him dies, so will her interest in attending Acton."

"What if her interest in Tyler doesn't die?"

"Then his will in her," Elena replied. Her jaw hurt from the way she was clenching it to control her voice from rising. "The truth is, when Gabby's heart is broken she'll finally grow up and figure out what's important."

"Ah, now we're getting to it. The Gospel According to Elena."

Oh, his voice was so deceptively, so sarcastically mild. She clenched her fists. "Go ahead and scoff."

"I'm not scoffing. I want to know what's 'important' to Elena O'Brien. What did growing up teach you?"

That was easy. "To count on no one but myself. To trust no one and nothing other than my own strength and my own sweat."

Though he was silent, the atmosphere seemed to grow heavy, charged with a tension that was almost electric. "Don't you really mean men?" he said. "That a woman shouldn't count on, trust a man?"

Elena tried to ignore the stormy feel that continued to gather in the small room. "That too," she muttered.

He popped out of the chair with such force that it slid back a foot. "Damn you. You really believe that, don't you?"

He stalked toward her, but she stood her ground and held her voice to a cool, methodical tone. "Why wouldn't I? Why wouldn't I think of my father and then every other male who has disappointed me— which would be all of them, by the way—and stay single and celibate?"

"Because you haven't?" he bit out. "In case I need to remind you, you *aren't* single and celibate."

She decided to ignore the celibate part. "There isn't a ring on my finger," she said. "There never has been, there never will be."

"You're trying to make me angry again."

The lines of his face had hardened and he didn't look anything like the charming, everybody-loves-him Logan that she was most familiar with. She turned away. "I don't know what you mean."

He grabbed her shoulder and turned her back. "You're not single, you're not celibate, Elena. You're with *me*."

She shook her head. "Don't," she said. "Don't."

"Don't what?" He tightened his fingers and gave her a little shake. "Don't make you say it?"

"I won't."

He jerked his hand away from her as if she burned him, or as if he was afraid of what he might do if he still touched her. "You're with me, Elena. We're together."

No! With him, together with Logan, would only lead to more heartache. She waved her hand. "It's a proximity thing, you know that. Under the same roof, past history, that's all."

"It's more than that."

"No." But she'd rather brave Gabby's bad mood than get further into this with Logan. Stomping over to her purse and tote bag, she slung them over her shoulder.

"We fell in love eleven years ago." Logan's eyes

were narrowed and his words clipped. "What if that happened again?"

"I'll never fall in love again," she said automatically. Instinctively. "I won't."

Logan froze, giving the temper in his voice an icy edge. "You won't, won't you?" he said slowly. "I can care about your day, your sister, I can care about you. I can take you to bed and make you mindless, but you'll never give your heart."

"Fool me once, shame on you," Elena retorted flippantly as she pivoted to leave the room. "Fool me twice—"

"No." He reached out to stay her movement and his fingers curled around the handles of the tote bag. It slid down her arm to catch at her elbow. "I'm an easygoing man," he ground out. "I like—"

"Things to be simple and uncomplicated," she finished for him. "So let's simplify things right now. I'm going upstairs." Ignoring the hand that still held her bag, she hurried forward.

"Damn it, Elena." He pulled back on the fabric handles to halt her movement.

She refused to look at him. "Let me go."

"I can't. I can't, damn it, because I'm in love with you."

Elena's head jerked up. Her gaze met his and he looked as stunned as she was—and still angry. "No," she said.

He was breathing hard, as if he'd run a very long way. "Yes. Yes. I'm in love with you and I think you're in love with me."

Shocked by his…his arrogance, she gaped at him. "I'm not in love with you. Never. Not in this lifetime. Not for a million dollars. Not in a million years." Realizing it was overkill as refusals went, she shut her mouth.

His jaw tightened and his voice was rough. "God, Elena, I just bared my soul here. I know you're scared, but the least you could do is give me the truth."

Now her temper flared. The truth? He wanted the truth? How about the truth that she never wanted to be hurt again? How about the truth that hurt was the only thing that could ever come of a man like Logan "loving" a woman like her? He would never truly love her—love her enough to stay.

But after years of practice, she found herself reaching for calm, for control. "The truth is, love makes a person weak and I won't be weak like that again." Grabbing the handles of her tote bag herself, she tried pulling them free of his hold. "The truth is, Logan, love doesn't last."

At that, his grasp loosened. The bag pitched, the contents slid forward, spilled. As the shoebox that was on top tumbled, it opened and Fred and Wilma executed a short free fall then smashed on the floor.

Both she and Logan stared at the mess. Then he shook his head, his anger still apparent in the harsh lines of his face and the hoarse sound of his voice. "Love doesn't last? Apparently neither does your ability to keep someone—and that includes yourself, Elena—safe."

And then, as she'd always known he would, he walked away again, leaving her feeling as empty and broken as the ruined eggs.

The good thing about being so exhausted, Elena decided on the afternoon of the prom, was that it numbed most emotions.

With the Garden-of-Eden decorations complete, last-minute worries over the dance barely tickled her mind. Disappointment over the ruined egg project was just a dull throb, even as she sat at the card table and turned the pages in her class journal to make the final entry. *Failure,* she wrote.

Somehow she'd failed Gabby too.

Unfortunately, that wasn't one of the numb emotions. It was sharp and painful and cut deeper each time Gabby passed Elena as she prepared for her big night. Wrapped in a robe, with her hair in hot curlers, her sister wandered out of the kitchen, a glass of ice water in her hand.

Elena tried smiling at her. "Is there anything I can do for you? Anything to help you get ready?"

"I'm fine." Gabby didn't shake the polite but cool attitude she'd had toward Elena since receiving the envelope from Acton two nights before. "Don't you have to get ready too?"

Elena shrugged. "I've got time. You and Tyler are meeting your friends for dinner. I don't have to be at the dance until seven."

Gabby frowned. "The two of you—you and Logan—aren't having dinner out first?"

Elena shook her head. She wasn't part of a "two," had really never been, unless you counted Gabby. "We're not, uh, dating anymore."

"No." Gabby's expression transformed from civility to concern as she crossed to the card table and pulled out the chair beside Elena's. "Are you all right?"

"Of course." She fiddled with the pen in her hand. "It's no big deal."

Gabby's hand covered hers. "Liar."

Elena thought better of meeting her sister's eyes. "Really. I'm really, really, really fine."

"Really." Gabby's voice held a touch of wryness.

Elena grimaced. She always erred on the side of overkill, it was true. "I'm okay, Gab."

Her sister squeezed her hand. "You're making me angry."

Elena glanced up. "I seem to be doing that a lot lately."

But it wasn't anger that was lighting Gabby's eyes. "Let me be a sister to you. Please."

"You're always my sister," Elena answered reasonably.

"No. I've let you mother me almost all our lives." She squeezed Elena's hand again. "And I needed a mother when I was little, I know that. But I'm grown up now. It's time for me to be a sister. A friend to you."

If she wasn't so exhausted, Elena thought, she wouldn't be so stupidly close to tears. "I don't want to lose you, Gabriellita,'' she heard herself whispering. Then she would have no one.

Gabby sniffed. ''You're not. You won't.''

''I never meant to make you feel used.'' Elena thought of Logan and his father and her heart squeezed with guilt. ''I was wrong to push you in a particular direction. I should listen better, but I...I just love you so much.''

''I'm going to *make* you listen from now on.''

They flew into each other's arms, the comforting embrace saying all the rest. After a few moments, Gabby sniffed again.

''Don't cry,'' Elena said, squeezing her sister tighter. ''It's going to be all right. Please don't cry.''

Gabby sniffed two more times, then drew in a deep breath. ''Okay. But there's nothing wrong with it, Elena. Sister-to-sister, let me tell you that a crying jag might do us both a world of good.''

Elena held her a little bit away. ''Sister-to-sister, we O'Brien women are ugly criers. We don't want puffy eyes and red noses tonight.''

When Gabby laughed, so did she. ''Sister-to-sister has a nice ring to it,'' Elena finally admitted. ''It might take me a little time to get used to all that that means, but I'll try.''

''It means we respect each other's decisions and love each other no matter what,'' Gabby replied. ''What's so hard about that?''

Sighing, Elena shook her head. ''I hope you have a daughter someday. It would only be fair.''

Gabby made a face. "Enough of that. Tell me what happened with you and Logan."

"He said he was in love with me, and I said I wasn't in love with him."

Gabby gaped at her. "No. No. You…you…what the heck were you thinking? Elena, how could you tell him that?"

This pain sliced at her too, sharp and deep, even though she'd broken up with Logan to protect herself from hurt. She drew away from Gabby. "You better hurry up and finish dressing. Tyler will be here soon."

"Elena—"

"I think this is where that 'respecting each other's decisions' comes in," she said dryly. "Drop it for now, Gabby, okay? Let's go take those curlers out."

After one last shake of her head, her sister didn't bring Logan up again. Elena helped Gabby into her dress and with her makeup and hair, and the forty-five minutes it took were the happiest the two of them had spent together in weeks. When Tyler knocked on the door, the look on his face when he saw Gabby sent Elena's heart to her throat.

Gabby appeared equally enchanted with Tyler. Elena could feel the giddiness of young love fizzing around them like bubbles in a glass of ginger ale. Her camera was waiting on the kitchen counter and the first time she looked through her viewfinder at the couple, the image sucked her breath away.

Through the objective eye of the lens, Elena clearly saw that Gabby was a woman. A woman who didn't need to be coddled as Elena had coddled Fred and Wilma. Gabby no longer depended on Elena for everything. She was ready to make her own choices, and two of them could very well be the Acton School and Tyler.

Blinking against the sting in her eyes, her finger clicked the shutter and then she called to the couple to make another pose. A knock sounded at the door and Tyler opened it to admit Laura Chase, Logan's mother.

Grinning at all of them, she held up her own camera. "As a mother only of sons, I never sent a daughter to the prom. May I?"

So Elena had a clicking companion, and better yet, someone to stand with her as Tyler and Gabby left the apartment behind. Mrs. Chase audibly sniffed.

"They grow up so fast, don't they?" she said.

Elena half-smiled, thinking that Logan's mother had only known Gabby for a few short weeks. Then she nodded. "But they do grow up."

She accepted that now.

Chapter Fourteen

The moment his mother bustled next door with her camera, Logan grabbed a beer and collapsed onto his couch. He'd worked with a crowbar all day—the rotting back wall of the shed behind the house would never be the same, not to mention the muscles in his shoulders—and it had worn him out.

Probably lingering after-effects of that damn virus. It had hit him hard two nights ago, right as he and Elena had called it quits. When she'd said she could never trust a man, that she would never love one, he'd suddenly felt feverish—hot and almost out of his head.

After a night without sleep he'd decided he was all better, though. Certainly he didn't care if she wanted to be single and celibate the rest of her life because—

God, no—he wasn't in love with her. That had been the virus talking and now he'd made a nearly complete recovery.

As she'd said, his attraction to her had been about proximity and that damn past of theirs. Questions about it had lingered in his mind for years and seeing her again had brought them to the forefront.

It was natural that he'd been compelled to uncover the truth. And yeah, her kisses were as brain-twisting as he'd remembered. Elena in bed was as extraordinary as he'd always fantasized.

But she was trouble, with a capital "T," and that was not for a man who, after years of entanglement had broken free to seek a simple—with a small "s"—life. Elena made him crazy, and he savored sanity, thank you very much.

A pounding on his door roused him from his thoughts and his seat. He opened the door to find his father on the other side. Only for an instant. In the next breath, Jonathon Chase pushed his way into the apartment.

"Laura," he called out. "I've had enough. It's time for you to stop this nonsense and come home."

Logan's eyebrows lifted. "She's uh, not here, Dad."

Jonathon sputtered a moment, then blinked. "Well, where is she?"

Ruining Gabby and Tyler's pre-prom moments wasn't something Logan would allow. "She'll be back soon." Then he held up his beer. "Would you like one?"

His father grunted and waved a dismissive hand, then dropped to Logan's couch. He was nattily dressed in his usual Saturday golf attire.

Logan sighed and sat on the other end of the couch. "How was your golf game today, Dad?"

"Don't ask."

"Ah, well." Logan tried to dredge up some sympathy, though the only thing he thought golf was good for were those low-voiced TV commentators. They'd lulled him into some of the best afternoon naps of his life.

Jonathon sank back against the couch cushions, his fingertips drumming a rhythm on his kneecaps. "How long will she be?"

Logan shrugged. "Don't know."

Jonathon frowned. "What the hell is going on in her mind?"

"Don't know."

Frowning deeper, his father rose to his feet to pace around Logan's living room. "I resent the way things are turning out in this family."

Logan just sipped from his bottle of beer.

"Your brother's married—I like that. But the rest, your mother and you, Logan, are confusing me."

"Why don't you just ask Mom, nicely, what's going on?" Logan suggested.

"I don't want to know what's going on! I want my life back, just the way it was."

Logan had some sympathy for that position until his father rounded on him. "I need you back at Chase Electronics."

Logan looked down at his beer bottle. "Oops. Empty." He stood up and escaped to the kitchen, thinking maybe he could stay in there awhile. It was always easier to avoid rather than confront his father.

Stalling, he opened the refrigerator and considered offering his dad a square of the lime gelatin and shredded carrot salad that sat, quivering with neglect, on the top shelf.

Bad idea, Logan decided. *One bite of that and he might not want Mom back.*

Then he heard the apartment door open.

"Jonathon!" his mother said.

"Laura."

The exchange of names was followed by a long, long silence. Fingers crossed, Logan walked out of the kitchen, hoping to find his parents in a reconciliatory embrace.

Maybe then his life could get back to normal.

But instead of forgiveness, understanding or even arguing, he found his parents in what appeared to be a stand-off. They were staring at each other, stony-faced.

Logan pinched the bridge of his nose, frustration and annoyance starting to pound like a headache in his brain. Breathing deeply, he tried to think good-natured, easygoing thoughts. Summer picnics. Kites flying in the sky. Puppies, kittens.

Only cauldrons of fire and pitchforks came to mind.

He inhaled another long breath. "Look who's here, Mom." When that garnered no response, he tried again. "Dad, Mom's back."

"This must stop," Jonathon finally bit out. His gaze moved from Logan's mother's face to Logan. "Today. This stops today."

"What?" Logan asked.

Jonathon pointed at his wife. "*You* are coming home." Then he pointed at Logan. "And *you* are coming back into the business."

Logan stared at his father, the flames in his mental cauldron leaping high to become a raging inferno. "What did you say?"

"I expect you back at your desk on Monday morning, 8:00 a.m. sharp."

Those flames rose higher, twisting and crackling, consuming in one instant a lifetime of laid-back diplomacy. "That's it," Logan said, stalking toward his parents. "I've had it."

His father blinked. "Logan?"

Logan's skin was hot, his emotions were hot, there was more heat crackling along the edges of his voice. "Dad, I admire you, I love you, but you're acting like a jackass and I'm not putting up with it anymore. Give up this ridiculous idea of yours. I'm not going back to Chase Electronics. I am going to proceed with my own business and my own life. I expect you never to bring up me working there again."

"Logan…" his mother started.

"And you!" He'd never before raised his voice to his mother. "You're mad at Dad. Well tell him why, for God's sake. Tell him what you want—*demand* it. Because he sure as hell isn't going to figure it out by himself."

They spoke at once. "Logan—"

"Furthermore, I am not Dear Abby and this is not the Lonely Hearts Rooming House." He took hold of one of their arms in each hand and directed them firmly toward the door. "Go home, Dad. Take Mom with you. And don't drag me into this again. I have my own problems."

His temper still running high and hot, he opened the door and—gently—threw his own parents out.

It felt damn good.

For something like five seconds. Then there was a hesitant knock on his door.

Gritting his teeth, he opened it an inch. His mother was peering at him.

"I need my purse," she said, an apology in her voice.

He merely swung the door open silently.

She hurried inside, shooting him a half smile. "I'm sorry, Logan. I know I put you in the middle and it *was* wrong of me." Lifting her purse from the coffee table, she looked at him again. "But you're right, you know. I told you that we need to demand what we want, and then I didn't do it. I've always made things much too easy for your father. I don't want him to get away with that anymore."

Logan ground his teeth together. "Don't tell that to me, Mom. Tell that to him."

She nodded, once, then headed for the door. "I intend to. But I hope…I hope you take your own advice, dear."

Logan frowned. "What are you talking about?"

"I'm no Dear Abby either. But look in your closet. I know you said you didn't need it anymore, but I hung something there that might provide some inspiration."

Elena inspected her image in the mirror. The dress she'd borrowed from Laura Chase was more sophisticated than a prom dress, and its strapless bodice and full skirt were the same color of blue as her eyes. She'd swept her hair into what Gabby called an "updo," then sifted through her jewelry box to find a sparkling necklace and matching earrings of faux sapphires.

The chic dress made the jewels—and Elena herself—much more elegant than they could be alone. She wondered what Logan would think—

No! She was supposed to be forgetting him.

It wasn't as if she imagined *he* was having trouble forgetting *her*.

Though once upon a time she'd probably believed that a man couldn't wipe her from his mind, it would have been before her father had left. Certainly before the senior prom, when Logan had blithely walked away. Every man she'd ever rebuffed since—and okay, maybe her initial prickly attitude toward them was always a test of sorts—had never bothered to persist, only confirming her mistrust.

And then, of course, two nights ago Logan had blithely walked away for the second time.

Curling her fingers into fists, Elena checked the clock. With a few more minutes before she had to leave, she might as well wipe a small task from her own mind. Telling Logan that she and Gabby were moving out the next day would be her first step in moving on from him.

The phone rang several times before he picked up. "Yeah, what?" he said abruptly.

"Um, sorry to bother you," Elena replied, suddenly regretting the impulse to call. "I...I wanted to let you know that Gabby and I will be packing up and moving back to our house tomorrow."

"Fine, fine." He sounded harried.

She told herself the casual dismissal didn't hurt. "Well, then. Thanks again."

A distant, strangled noise came over the phone.

Elena hesitated. "Are you okay?"

There was a pause and then he spoke, his voice clear now, but no less rushed-sounding. "I'm busy. I had to run out for something and now I'm in a hell of a hurry. You caught me straight from the shower."

Naked. She thought of his big body with its hard, sleek muscles. She thought of the ways he'd used it to make love to her, sometimes gentle, sometimes so passionate that she shivered just thinking about it.

Swallowing hard, she tore the mental image into a thousand tiny pieces. "Well, I'm sorry. I'll let you—"

"No, no. I'm glad you called. I wanted to tell you something."

It was Saturday night. He had just showered.

He was going to tell her he had a date, she thought.

Her stomach lurched, buffeted by waves of pain and jealousy. "I—"

"My family is your typical Anglo-Saxon, cold-as-cucumbers-in-Jell-O crowd."

She blinked. "Jell-O?"

"Never mind." He mumbled a curse at a missing black sock, then spoke clearly again. "The point is, what I felt for you eleven years ago, Elena, was hotter, edgier, more passionate than any kind of male-female relationship I'd ever seen or experienced. I ran from it. From you. And kept running from both until you showed up in my world again."

"You like things simple," Elena replied dully, not understanding why he wanted to rehash this now. "Easy."

"But simple and easy doesn't always mean happy," he said. "Even though I thought it did. I thought it was smart to run from passion. I called it 'the beast,' you know. But now, now I realize it's the best of what you release in me. It's what makes me feel alive."

"What?" Elena took the phone from her ear, stared at it, then brought it back. "What are you saying?"

"I'm saying, open your door."

"What?"

"Open your door."

Still confused and going cold all over, Elena did as he said. And there he stood, in a black tuxedo, a cordless phone in one hand and a corsage box in the other.

She could only stare at him and try not to tremble. "What…what are you doing here?" she finally said.

"We have a date, remember?"

He'd come back.

Turning his wrist, he checked his watch. "7:00 p.m. on the dot."

He was right on time.

"I love you."

And he loved her. Oh! No! No, she couldn't let herself believe—

"Go ahead, try to doubt me," Logan said, stepping forward even as she retreated. "Go ahead and try to push me out of your life. But you won't get away with it this time, Elena."

"I never pushed you out." She continued to scurry back, afraid to let him close, afraid that he would make her weak again and hurt her even more.

Then her back bumped against the wall. Suddenly his hands were empty except for a wrist corsage of white baby roses and gauzy, sapphire-blue ribbon. She tried to dodge him, but her reflexes were still slowed by the surprise of having him here. It took just a moment for him to capture her hand and then slide the flowers over her cold fingers and onto her arm.

They both stared at it and Elena tried to pretend that the rose petals weren't clearly shaking.

His warm fingers squeezed her cold ones. "That was a long time coming," he said.

It was the soft note in his voice that finally woke her up. It was a soft, seductive, treacherous note that tried to slip beneath her defenses. It tried to make her not only *feel* sixteen again, but *be* sixteen again, when love—and Logan—were fairy tales she still let herself believe in.

"No," she said, whipping her hand free of his. She couldn't set herself up for another fall. She wouldn't. "I don't want this. I don't want to go to the prom with you."

Crossing his arms over his chest, he narrowed his eyes. "Too bad. Because I'll be damned if I'm going to let you go to the stupid dance alone and then hear for the *next* eleven years that I stood you up again."

She went from apprehension to outrage in a split second. "I wouldn't—"

"Oh, yes. Yes, you would."

Elena felt her face go red. She felt her whole body flame, as if the very pores of her skin were exuding long-suppressed Latin temperament. *"Cochino."*

His lips twitched. "I'm going to assume that was a compliment."

He was laughing at her! Fueled by the thought, her temper leaped. "Go away," she spat out.

His shoes seemed to find root in the floor as he regarded her with almost clinical interest. "Never."

"Logan—"

"Never."

Panicky now, she stamped her foot and didn't even feel ashamed of the childish action. Then she yanked the corsage off her arm and held it high.

His hand instantly closed over her raised wrist. "There. There's the Elena I've been waiting for."

She tried to wound him with a look.

It only caused his lips to twitch again. "Go ahead," he said. "Get angry. Get really angry."

She stamped her foot once more and tried to pull free of him. "Why are you doing this?"

He brought her hand to his mouth, then brushed his lips across her knuckles. "So that I can see the real you, the fiery, passionate Elena that I love."

"What are you talking about?" Frustrated tears were stinging the corners of her eyes and she'd rather die than cry in front of him. "I'm *mad* at you!"

"Mad enough to marry me?"

Her heart jolted and her gaze jerked up to his.

His face was serious now and his golden eyes watchful. But he was teasing her. He had to be teasing her.

"I should," she whispered, her voice lost somewhere between terror and unwarranted, silly joy. "I should say yes and then let you suffer through a wild, tempestuous marriage."

The guarded look in his eyes evaporated and he smiled. It was that easygoing, charming Logan smile, but she sensed something new in it, an intent, a determination, that had her nerves dancing along the surface of her skin.

"I dare you," he said.

Again, her heart jolted in her chest. "*Dare* me?"

Mio Dios. Logan hadn't forgotten her. He hadn't stood her up. He'd *shown* up. On time. Because he loved her. To ask her to marry him.

And he'd done it in just this way, because he knew

her well enough to know she'd never be able to resist a challenge. Some new emotion bubbled through her.

It wasn't passion, she'd always felt that for Logan.

It wasn't love...that she was familiar with too, because he'd been her first love and now it looked as if he was going to be her last.

This new feeling was...trust.

Trust that this man would do whatever he must to have her. And because of that, she could trust that her heart would always be safe with him.

Finally, after all the years, the fight, the fear ran out of her.

"Oh, Logan." She threw her arms around his neck. "Oh, Logan, I love you."

He caught her to him. "I demand it."

There was such certainty and such happiness in his eyes that her heart pounded harder. "And I'll marry you."

"I demand that too."

Then he kissed her, and Elena heard the strangest, sweetest sound. She heard it later too, as Logan led her to the center of the auditorium for their long-postponed prom dance.

He looked down at her quizzically. "Do you hear something?" he asked. "Besides the song, I mean."

She smiled, and across the room caught Gabby's eye to blow her a kiss. "Yep, I do."

His arms closed around her. "Well, what is it?"

Elena ran her gaze around the exotic decorations, then she closed her eyes to savor the moment. "This is Paradise, isn't it?"

The blissful voices she heard sounded just like her mother's and grandmother's. *We did it, Mama. See, Nana?* Your girls are happy.

Elena laid her cheek against Logan's shoulder. ''It's the angels singing.''

* * * * *

SPECIAL EDITION™
&
SILHOUETTE *Romance*

present a new series about the proud,
passion-driven dynasty

THE
COLTONS

**You loved the California Coltons, now discover
the Coltons of Black Arrow, Oklahoma.
Comanche blood courses through their veins,
but a brand-new birthright awaits them....**

WHITE DOVE'S PROMISE by Stella Bagwell (7/02, SE#1478)

THE COYOTE'S CRY by Jackie Merritt (8/02, SE#1484)

WILLOW IN BLOOM by Victoria Pade (9/02, SE#1490)

THE RAVEN'S ASSIGNMENT by Kasey Michaels (9/02, SR#1613)

A COLTON FAMILY CHRISTMAS by Judy Christenberry,
Linda Turner and Carolyn Zane (10/02, Silhouette Single Title)

SKY FULL OF PROMISE by Teresa Southwick (11/02, SR#1624)

THE WOLF'S SURRENDER by Sandra Steffen (12/02, SR#1630)

*Look for these titles
wherever Silhouette books are sold!*

Silhouette®
Where love comes alive™

MONTANA MAVERICKS

One of Silhouette Special Edition's most popular series returns with three sensational stories filled with love, small-town gossip, reunited lovers, a little murder, hot nights and the best in romance:

HER MONTANA MAN
by Laurie Paige
(ISBN#: 0-373-24483-5)
Available August 2002

BIG SKY COWBOY
by Jennifer Mikels
(ISBN#: 0-373-24491-6)
Available September 2002

MONTANA LAWMAN
by Allison Leigh
(ISBN#: 0-373-24497-5)
Available October 2002

*True love is the only way to beat the heat
in Rumor, Montana....*

Silhouette®

Where love comes alive™

Silhouette®

SPECIAL EDITION™

Coming in August 2002,
from Silhouette Special Edition and

CHRISTINE RIMMER,

the author who brought you the popular series

CONVENIENTLY YOURS,

brings her new series

THE SONS OF CAITLIN BRAVO

Starting with

HIS EXECUTIVE SWEETHEART
(SE #1485)...

One day she was the prim and proper executive assistant...
the next, Celia Tuttle fell hopelessly in love with her boss,
mogul Aaron Bravo, bachelor extraordinaire. It was clear he
was never going to return her feelings, so what was a girl to
do but get a makeover—and try to quit. Only suddenly,
was Aaron eyeing his assistant in a whole new light?

And coming in October 2002, MERCURY RISING,
also from Silhouette Special Edition.

**THE SONS OF CAITLIN BRAVO: Aaron, Cade and Will.
They thought no woman could tame them.
How wrong they were!**

Silhouette®

Where love comes alive™

SSESCB

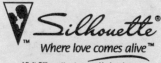

Where royalty and romance go hand in hand...

The series continues in Silhouette Romance with these unforgettable novels:

HER ROYAL HUSBAND
by Cara Colter
on sale July 2002 (SR #1600)

THE PRINCESS HAS AMNESIA!
by Patricia Thayer
on sale August 2002 (SR #1606)

SEARCHING FOR HER PRINCE
by Karen Rose Smith
on sale September 2002 (SR #1612)

And look for more Crown and Glory stories in SILHOUETTE DESIRE starting in October 2002!

Available at your favorite retail outlet.

SINTMAG

Silhouette Books is proud to present:

Going to the Chapel

Three brand-new stories
about getting that special man to the altar!

featuring

USA Today bestselling author

SHARON SALA

It Happened One Night...that Georgia society belle
Harley June Beaumont went to Vegas—and woke up married!
How could she explain her hunk of a husband to
her family back home?

Award-winning author
DIXIE BROWNING

Marrying a Millionaire...was exactly what Grace McCall was
trying to keep her baby sister from doing. Not that Grace had
anything against the groom—it was the groom's arrogant
millionaire uncle who got Grace all hot and bothered!

National bestselling author
STELLA BAGWELL

The Bride's Big Adventure...was escaping her handpicked
fiancé in the arms of a hot-blooded cowboy! And from the
moment Gloria Rhodes said "I do" to her rugged groom, she
dreamed their wedded bliss would never end!

Available in July at your favorite retail outlets!

Silhouette®

Where love comes alive™

COMING NEXT MONTH

#1483 HER MONTANA MAN—Laurie Paige
Montana Mavericks
It had been eight long years since small-town mayor Pierce Dalton
chose work over love. Then pretty forensic specialist Chelsea Kearns
came back into his life—and his heart. Pierce hoped that one last fling
with Chelsea would burn out their still-simmering flame once and for
all. But they hadn't counted on the strength of their passion...or an
unexpected pregnancy!

#1484 THE COYOTE'S CRY—Jackie Merritt
The Coltons
Golden girl Jenna Elliott was all wrong for hardworking Native
American sheriff Bram Colton, *right?* She was rich, privileged and,
most shocking of all, *white*. But Bram couldn't help but feel desire for
Jenna, his grandmother's new nurse—and Jenna couldn't help but feel
the same way. Would their cultural differences tear them apart or build
a long-lasting love?

#1485 HIS EXECUTIVE SWEETHEART—Christine Rimmer
The Sons of Caitlin Bravo
Celia Tuttle's whole world went haywire when she realized she was
in love...with her boss! Tycoon Aaron Bravo had his pick of willing,
willowy women, so why would he ever fall for his girl-next-door
secretary? But then shy Celia—with a little help from Aaron's
meddling mom—figured out a way to *really* get her boss's
attention....

#1486 THE HEART BENEATH—Lindsay McKenna
Morgan's Mercenaries: Ultimate Rescue
When a gigantic earthquake ripped apart Southern California, marines
Callie Evans and Wes James rushed to the rescue. But the two tough-
as-nails lieutenants hadn't expected an undeniable attraction to each
other. Then the aftershocks began. And this time it was Callie in need
of rescue—and Wes was determined to save the woman he'd fallen
for!

#1487 PRINCESS DOTTIE—Lucy Gordon
Barmaid Dottie Heben...a *princess?* One day the zany beauty was
slinging drinks, the next day she learned she was the heiress to a
throne. All Dottie had to do was get a crash course in royal relations.
But the one man assigned to give her "princess lessons" was the same
man she'd just deposed...former prince Randolph!

#1488 THE BOSS'S BABY BARGAIN—Karen Sandler
Brooding millionaire Lucas Taylor longed for a child—but didn't have
a wife. So when his kindhearted assistant, Allie Dickenson, came to
him for a loan, the take-charge businessman made her a deal: marriage
in exchange for money. Could their makeshift wedding lead to a once-
in-a-lifetime love that healed past wounds?